The Curses We Keep

Dakota J. Miller

Contents

To the darkness that dares us to know ourselves,
and the stories we weave from its depths.

Prologue

The woods lay silent, a black mouth swallowing sound. Pines stood jagged and skeletal against a sky bruised with dusk, their branches reaching upward as though clawing for the last veins of light. Spanish moss hung in long, gray shrouds that swayed in the still air, heavy with damp. Drops fell slow to the earth, each bead glinting like a tear suspended in its fall before breaking the mud with a soft patter. The rhythm drummed through her skull as if the forest itself possessed a pulse.

Thickened air, sharp with resin and the sour rot of leaves half-swallowed by the earth. Their decay whispered beneath her feet, a slow gurgle winding through the quiet, curling into her lungs until she breathed the forest's sickness. Roots jutted from the soil, slick with moisture, glistening as though the land itself bled. Strips of bark peeled away and caught the faint wind that moaned through the trees, a thin sound that climbed her spine and urged her deeper.

The old hag moved with care, her steps halting, her weight dragging in the mud. The cloak about her shoulders hung heavy, its hem soaked and torn by thorns. Each rip made a small sound, a sigh against the quiet. Behind her trailed a rope, coarse hemp, thick and frayed. It rasped over the ground as it followed, taken from a wagon long ago, once reins guided by a hand she had loved. What was a lifeline then had become a burden, a shadow that followed her wherever she went.

Her breath came in shallow bursts, pale wisps trembling in the cold. Her chest ached beneath the weight of the air. She had entered the wood where the frost still lingered, and the river's murmur wound through the trees like a warning. Moss brushed her face, damp and cold as a dead hand urging her back. But she pressed on, stumbling over roots that caught her boots and clawed her ankles. Mud sucked at her soles with greedy lips. Each step drew her deeper, as if the forest bent to watch.

The rope snagged, caught fast in a root's grip, and jerked her backward. She stumbled, her arm shuddering from the strain. Mud clung to the hemp, dark and thick, and the weight of it sank into her gut. She freed it with trembling hands. Her fingers were gnarled and cracked, her nails rimed with dirt. She tugged the rope loose and it rasped wetly against bark. The sound reminded her of her own pulse.

Her face was a map of years carved by grief and sun. Beneath her thin skin the bones jutted, her color leached by time and cold. She lifted her hands before her, turning them in the dim light. Once they had been small and sure, deft with the reins, steady in their work. She remembered the child's hands that had learned knots at a father's side, the young woman's hands that had tied rope in defiance, the mother's hands that had reached toward flames and found only smoke. Those memories blurred together until they belonged to no one she knew. Now her fingers shook, dragging the rope behind her through the muck while the forest closed in, its shadows writhing like breath.

Whispers of the townsfolk still clung to her, thin as cobwebs but impossible to tear away. They spoke of curses and foul power, of a woman too long alone in the woods. Their words followed her through the trees like smoke. They had not seen the things she had, the flicker at the corner of the eye, the glint of steel, the flash of fire. She had tried to warn them, tried to shield them. But her cries were met with stones, her pleas with prayers muttered through clenched teeth. They saw only a witch, a shadow to cast out.

Her heart felt like a stone she could no longer bear. The rope grew heavier in her hands as she moved. Mud coated its coils, the noose she had carried in silence, tracing it through years she could not name. Faces returned to her in the dark: the laughing child by the wagon, the same face streaked with terror. Each memory pulled at her until she thought the weight of them would drag her down.

The forest stirred. The wind sharpened, its voice rising through the branches. Twigs snapped like bones underfoot.

She came to a hollow, a place where the ground sank low and the air hung thick with rot. Roots twisted like veins through the mud, pulsing faintly beneath her touch. The scent of decay stung her nose and filled her mouth with the taste of iron. She swallowed and steadied herself.

She sank to her knees. The rope pooled beside her, wet and heavy, gleaming in the weak light like a serpent poised to strike. Her breath trembled as she looked down at it. Her fingers moved without will, lifting the coils she had stolen hours before, taken from trusting hands. The rope's fibers were rough against her skin, darkened by age and use. She ran her hands over its knots and felt the strength still held within them. Then she rose, slow and deliberate, and looped it over a low branch. The bark tore her palms until thin lines of blood slipped down her wrists. The color shone dark against the pale rope.

She placed the noose around her neck. The fibers scratched her skin. Her breath came shallow again, clouding the cold air. She stood still for a moment, her boots sinking in the wet earth that seemed to hold her there.

This was her offering, the only act left to her. The forest pressed close, the air waiting. She drew in a long breath, let it shiver out, and stepped forward. The branch gave a low groan, the sound of wood surrendering to weight. The rope tightened, bit, and eased. Her body swung, light now, turning slowly in the chill air. Droplets fell from the rope and struck the mud below. Each spark of water caught the dying light and vanished.

The forest dimmed around her. The trees blurred, their edges softening into black. A coolness spread through her veins, not peace but something like it. She had sought to end the circle that bound her, but even as the world fell away, she knew it would not release her.

Faces flickered in the dark, gentle at first, then twisted in terror. Hands reached for her through smoke and blood. Their voices rose and broke against her fading breath. The forest leaned close, the moss above her swaying like shrouds over a grave eager to close. The wind lifted again, carrying a long, low wail that wound through the trees.

The witch in the woods,
a shadow of her own making,
hung between earth and sky,
caught forever in the dark she had called home.

Chapter 1

The wagon jolted over rutted earth. Its creaks answered the sea Earnest York had left behind, that fickle beast that swallows men and keeps no ledger. Salt still seemed to cling to his skin. His hands, toughened by years on wet decks, held the reins until his knuckles blanched. Calluses rasped the leather as he guided the horse through Charleston's dusk-soaked outskirts.

Trees lifted their black arms against a dimming sky. Veils of moss swayed, brushing his cheek with cold damp as the light thinned. The air pressed heavy and warm. It pooled in his lungs with the tang of silt and resin, and something sour beneath, like a grave disturbed.

Beside him, Iris sat rigid. She cradled their daughter, Cassandra, whose head lay against her shoulder. The girl slept in starts, breath soft and even, a small shelter Earnest envied.

He scanned the timberline where shadows gathered in the hollows. The forest carried a rhythm he recognized from bad water and a falling barometer, the hush before a break.

The sea had written itself into him. Nets and lines had scored his forearms. Old rope burns mapped the places where the deck had heaved and the rigging snapped. He kept those memories locked down with a seaman's habit, but they moved in him all the same.

The wagon rattled. His fingers brushed a coil of hemp tied to the board, a length saved from a storm off Virginia. He had lashed himself to the mast that night while the ship came apart, the rope cutting his wrists until they bled. Tom went over the rail laughing at the wrong second, and the wave took him. Eli shouted once and then the wind swallowed the sound. After the blow passed and rain thinned to needles, Earnest had cut himself loose and watched gray water fold and unfold. Gulls circled the place where men sank. Their cries followed him south like a hymnal he never asked to learn.

"Steady now," he said, more to himself than to the horse. Hooves beat a dull time. Leaves whispered. Somewhere a twig cracked, clean and close. He turned his head. Moss lifted and fell as if a body had just passed through and left nothing behind.

Iris leaned forward. Her hand brushed the worn pouch at her waist where she kept her simples. Yarrow and sage rustled as she moved. Her gaze cut up the road and then into the woods, searching like a blade for a seam.

"It's too quiet," she said, voice low.

Earlier, a mile back, she had knelt at a ditch and picked a few sprigs that should have been healthy. Their edges had already curled black despite the heat. Stems snapped brittle in her fingers as if a frost had crept where no frost belonged.

"The air's wrong here," she had told him then. Now she crushed a leaf and lifted it. Green stained her fingertips. A bitter reek rose sharp enough to sting her nose. She wiped the color on her skirt, and it stayed like a mark.

"It's too thick. Hard to breathe. Feels like something is watching." She had tucked the wilted sprigs away, brow furrowed and muttered about signs she had seen north of Danvers: plants that soured before storms, a stillness before a scream, sickrooms where she had stitched torn flesh while fever burned too hot.

A branch popped deeper in the trees. She started and set her feet as if to meet weather.

Earnest clucked the horse on. "There's something queer about this place. But I ain't never seen a siren, and I ain't about to say the air's alive. Superstition, that's all."

His grip found the rope again, the coil a weight that steadied him while the forest's pulse seemed to rise.

They had stopped twice before dusk. First at a narrow creek where he had checked the axle. The wood had groaned with the load and showed a splinter from a jolt two days back. Iris had sifted roots and leaves along the bank and found a cluster of sage gone gray and sour to the touch. It crumbled in her palm.

"Was that a deer we heard?" she asked him.

A deer places four steps, not one, he thought, but said nothing. He was a man who believed the ocean had a temper. He did not believe in ghosts. Still, the feeling of eyes on their backs had ridden with them since noon, and they had passed enough native hunters on the road to earn a little watchfulness.

"That or them injuns watching us," he said. "No call to be spooked."

He had tightened the rope then. The hemp bit his palm, and the old habit calmed him.

"Time to move on," he said, and they had climbed back up. The wagon creaked. Far off, a river sounded louder than it should, a steady growl that worked under the trees and settled into his bones.

The second stop came in a thin place where the pines opened to a patch of sky the color of pewter. He watered the horse. Steam rose from its breath as the heat bled out of the day. A wavering cry rode the wind and was gone. Iris stiffened and drew Cassandra closer. Earnest clicked his tongue and set them moving again.

At the edge of the clearing Iris had knelt by another patch of plants. Yarrow drooped black. The stems were soft and rotten between her fingers, a rot she had seen once in a Danvers field before the first accusations.

"It's an omen," she said, standing. She wiped her hands on her apron and left a green-brown smear. "Feels like the ground is waiting to swallow something. I don't know what."

When the road bent toward the water they drew up. The river took the last light and cut it fine. Foam turned and broke on the current. Patterns opened and closed as if an eye were learning to blink.

Earnest dropped to the bank. Wet soil took his weight. He set out the blankets, the dented kettle, and the same coil of rope, still sound though the fibers had lifted with age. His hand passed over it by habit.

He glanced toward the timber again. Shadows lay thick where the moss hung low. A chill came that did not belong to the hour, the kind a man feels after another man slips beneath a wave and does not rise.

"Settle in," he said. The sailor's edge in his voice had not dulled with land. He touched the whalebone knife at his belt, its curve cool under his thumb, the promise it carried from Danvers still unbroken.

Iris stepped down and tore her skirt on a splinter. She looked to the river, listening to that heavy rush that always sounded like a choice. She steadied Cassandra as the girl stirred.

Cassandra blinked at the dim. Dust and damp tangled her hair. Shadows swam in her gazelike shapes just beneath the surface of a pond.

"Are we there, Father?" she asked.

"Nearly, Cassie." He tried to smile and failed at the edges. He pointed toward the water. "Fetch us some. Pail's there. Don't wander, hear?"

She nodded and slipped away. The pail swung in her hand. Dusk swallowed her faster than it should. Grass gave to bare soil, then to sand, then to cool mud that took her weight.

The ground softened. Mud seeped through the leather and chilled her toes. The river worked in her ears until it was all she heard. Her father's tales named water treacherous, and now it sounded true.

She knelt. The pail scraped stone. The current churned and stretched her reflection until the dark took her eyes. A girl she barely knew looked back.

Her thoughts bent toward forbidden doors. What if there were power in the places adults warned against. She pushed the thought aside and bile rose with the memory of names thrown at her in Danvers.

"Witch's spawn. Devil's child."

Her mother had hushed such talk with a look. Her father had answered with his fists. Memory did not always obey. The river snarled. The woods pressed close. A stick broke behind her.

She turned. Water slopped over her hands and went cold to the sleeves.

A cloaked figure stood on her side of the river. It was gaunt. The hood shadowed a face leached of color. Eyes black as sockets fixed on her. Tears had carved lines down sunken cheeks and caught the last light in a way that made the wet look like metal. The mouth opened and pulled wide. Teeth showed.

A hand lifted, shaking. Split nails. Skin like parchment. The fingers curled toward her, slow and pleading.

No sound came, only that stare, raw and lost, seeing past her at something she could not name. The body had settled into angles that spoke of long ruin.

"Who are you?" Cassandra whispered. The verse rose in her mind unbidden, *Thou shalt not suffer a witch,* and her world narrowed to that reaching hand.

The figure broke into a jag of laughter and then forced a single word.

"No."

It came up from a place that had worn all the edges off. The sound filled the pines.

Her heart struck hard against her ribs. *It knows me. It sees me,* she thought.

She slid to the right. Mud took her heel. The figure shifted with the same broken timing. Wet leaves flew from the sweep of its cloak. Fear closed her throat until breath rasped.

She backed away. The figure came on. Branches cracked. Its eyes held her like a pin.

She ran. Limbs snatched at her shawl. Cloth tore. Sweat chilled her skin. The river sucked at her boots where the bank dipped low.

The cry rose again behind her, long and ragged, and chased her through the trees.

"No."

Her lungs burned. She looked back and nearly fell. The hand lifted higher, still shaking, the fingers closing and opening as if working air. Tears slicked the ruin of that face. The eyes sank deeper. She saw herself in it, older and broken, and the sight stole her breath.

She cut left. Roots hooked her foot. Brambles tore her forearms and warmed her sleeves. Panic beat a fast time in her ears.

Another wail clawed the sky.

She saw the river through the trunks and the pale strip of bank. She sprinted. The figure lunged. Cloak flared. For a heartbeat the world went black at the edges.

"Help!"

Her voice cracked and tore. She jumped. Cold closed over her. The current took her legs, then her breath. She grabbed for anything and found a slick root. Nails tore but held. She hauled herself onto the mud while the cry behind her thinned and went strange, like choice turning to fate.

She lay there shivering and smeared with river silt. The woods settled by degrees. The echo of that voice hung in the trees and would not lift.

Shapes formed at the edge of the dark. Cloaks moved. Beads took the last light and gave it back dull. Footfalls rustled leaves with a steady measure that worked into her bones. She tightened both hands around the branch she had used to pull herself free. Blood ran from her knuckles and pooled in the mud while the figures came on, slow and sure, eyes catching what little glow remained.

Chapter 2

Night gathered at Charleston's edge with a low, river-borne murmur. Wind moved in the understory and set the leaves whispering. A small figure hurried through the brush, cloak frayed and flapping, boots lifting damp litter that stuck to the leather. Her breath showed white in the chill, brief puffs that fled as soon as they rose. Roots and thorn canes made a little prison of the path while, ahead, a pale twitch of motion slipped from trunk to trunk and was gone. The river kept its hum, a steady note that worked through the trees like a lure.

Her steps hit a tangle of roots and checked. Cold moss slid along her arm. The quiet collapsed, replaced by a slow scrape circling the pines, cloth on bark, branches giving a little under weight that meant intent. She stood still, chest lifting and falling, eyes trying to sort shape from dark. A taller shadow slid free of the timber, hooded, its tread dry and certain. "Who's there?" she tried, barely more than breath. The shape came fast. A rough hand closed on her forearm and pinched through the cloak. A bitter rag found her mouth. Her cry thinned to a whimper as her heels kicked leaves and dirt into brief arcs.

The figure hauled her deeper. The river's note swelled, and the trees seemed to lean. She beat at the arm that held her, knuckles scraping skin. The grip did not give. A low chuckle came from the hood, slow and pleased, a hunter's sound.

They reached a shallow hollow slick with mud. The air held a metallic tang. The figure pinned her with one knee. Cold soaked through her cloak and bit her back. From the cloak came a clay bowl, rim stained dark; then a curved knife blinked in the last of the light.

Her eyes widened. The knife hovered, then lowered. A careful line opened along her wrist. Heat ran to her hand and fell into the bowl in soft taps, a sound like rain beginning. The knife worked again, practiced and calm. Red slid down her arm and painted her skin. Teeth glinted under the hood. Flesh lifted, and the mouth moved. A whisper followed, hoarse with ownership. The bowl began to fill.

"Cassandra!" A man's call broke across the trees, frayed with fear. The girl bucked. "Cassandra!" A woman's voice followed, nearer and urgent. She tried to answer. The rag swallowed it. Nails tore as she clawed at roots for any noise that might carry. The knee ground harder into her ribs. Her body went still by inches.

“No one’s coming,” the figure said, the words thick with breath. Blood poured faster into the clay. Her limbs twitched and slowed. A small glass vial appeared; the killer tipped it and caught what they could, stoppered it, and slid it away. Another pass of the blade hovered above her chest and stopped. A long breath. The hand eased. The figure stood, tucked the prize inside the cloak, and stepped back into the trees. The river lifted its sound and covered the last thread of her gasp.

Earnest broke wet twigs with every stride. His lantern swung and sent thin light across trunks and low hollows. Damp climbed his coat and settled in his lungs with the same heavy feel that had lived in him on bad water. Iris kept his pace. Her breathing came quick and shallow. Her hands worked at her sides as if reaching for the little pouch that had mended so much and now promised nothing.

Cassandra should have returned by now. The absence gnawed and opened an old place they had tried to leave in Massachusetts. The forest spoke in small snaps and leaf-hiss, sounds that felt arranged. Earnest lifted his voice. “Cassandra!” The shout hit the trees and thinned. He swung the lantern wider and washed light across black mouths of hollow and notch. Memory sent up Tom’s grin, Eli’s single shout; the ocean takes fast. This ground felt patient. It chewed.

“She’s never strayed this long,” Iris said. She scanned the drift of moss and the seams between trunks. Her fingers, stained green from earlier, touched her skirt and then closed to keep them from shaking. “Not since...” She left the name of that town unsaid. She steadied her breath and moved on.

“We’ll find her,” Earnest said. He made his voice a tool and tried to believe it. The lantern picked up water through the trees, a flat shine and a moving edge.

“There,” Iris said, pointing.

The bank showed itself, swallowing a dull moon in broken skin. Foam worked and turned. Earnest lifted the light and sent it over the mud. The wagon’s wheel had settled deeper. A board creaked under his boot. Something else snagged his eye.

“Rope’s gone,” he said, low. The place he had left it was bare. The reins hung loose where they should have been bound.

Iris looked toward the timber and then forced her gaze back. “Storm must have taken it,” she said, the words plain and unbelieved.

He walked the beam along the bank. Small prints scarred the mud in wild lines toward the water. Toes dug deep. The surface showed churn and drag. “Cassie’s,” he said, kneeling. The mud was cold against his fingers. The marks were fresh.

Iris gripped his sleeve. She followed the track to a low froth at the edge and swallowed. A snapped branch hung close by, sap bright on the break. “Earnest.” She turned to a trunk and pointed. Gouges raked the bark in wide, crude slashes. Not saw. Not antler. Fresh sap bled along the cuts.

"No man," he said, rising. "No beast I know." He had seen what hooves and claws and iron leave. This was none of them.

Iris stepped nearer and held her hand over the marks without touching. Sap strung to her fingertip when she drew back. She crouched at the waterline, ran two fingers through a dark smear, and lifted them. Red shone thin in the lantern's glare. "Not hers," she said, the words half breath, half plea. She faced the current where a faint tint marred the foam.

A cry cut through the trees, high, human, and brief. Wind took the end of it. Earnest turned, lantern high. Moss moved as if a body had passed at speed between the boles. "What was that?" he said, voice hardening. He raked the light through the gaps and found only changeable dark.

Iris's breath showed in pale bursts. She peered past the churn and the gouged tree. "Close," she whispered. She edged forward, boots slipping. The echo faded into wind-voice and the slow drip of sap.

Earnest walked the bank, calling, "Cassandra!" The river spread black and wide, breaking the lantern's reach into ruined coins. Where the ripples crossed, something troubled the surface and then went flat.

Iris called too, and each answerless return scraped her raw. Cold got into the bones the way seawater does after a man goes under. Leaves stirred behind them with a steady tread that did not belong to wind.

Figures stepped from the trees, hides dark with river damp, beadwork winking once in the lantern's swing. An elder lifted his palm and set the group at a distance. A young woman stood beside him, hair bound with river shells, eyes steady.

She spoke in slow English. "Your daughter is safe. We pulled her from the water." She turned and repeated it in her tongue. The elder answered without softening his gaze. She faced Earnest again. "I am Tala. I will speak for my father."

Earnest did not lower the lantern. "Where is she." It was not a question so much as a test. His knuckles tightened on the handle. "And why touch what is not yours."

Tala watched the elder, then said, "By our fire. She was drowning." The words were plain. "We could not leave her."

"Could," Earnest said. "Many would." His eyes slid over the hunters as if counting hands and knives. "I know your kind." Iris's fingers pressed his sleeve, warning.

Wind came off the river with the first scent of rain. Tala tipped her chin toward the dark beyond. "Come. For tonight." She listened to the elder's low reply and added, "My father allows standing by our flames. Not more."

They moved through close growth where old spiral cuts and slashes caught the light on the trunks. Tala named them softly in her language and then in English, marks that hold stories, and walked on. The hunters moved quiet and sure. Earnest kept the lantern high, set to find fault. The elder did not look at him.

The village showed as a pocket of fire on raised ground. Dugout canoes rested with noses in the mud below, interiors charred smooth. Cane walls took the fireglow; palmetto thatch turned down against weather. Cassandra sat wrapped in a blanket. She rose when she saw them and fell into Iris's arms. Iris smoothed wet hair from her face and breathed.

Earnest crouched and looked over the girl's hands and eyes, then glanced up. "You pulled her out." He made the thanks for Tala, not the elder.

The elder spoke a short sentence that held no welcome. Tala translated, careful. "My father says the river gives and takes. Tonight, it gave. He says it was my choice to send men in."

Earnest's mouth twitched. "So the chief would have watched her drown."

Tala's face did not change. She listened to another low answer and said, "He says strangers bring storms and quarrels. He keeps peace by his roofs. Your trouble is yours. Tonight is an exception."

Cloud lowered. A scatter of hard drops struck the canoes and palmetto. Iris looked at the path they had come by and at the sky. "If we leave now, we will be swallowed by it."

The elder spoke again. Tala's voice stayed even. "You will not cross the woods in this wind. Stand by our eaves until morning. Not inside."

"We have our own camp," Earnest said. "We will go when the rain eases."

"He says you go at first light," Tala answered. "That is enough talk."

Earnest stared at the elder as if measuring him on a yard of rope. "We will be gone with the sun," he said, and it was not quite a promise.

Lightning blinked far off. Rain thickened, drumming the canoe hulls. Tala gestured to the edge of a shelter where the palmetto ran a clean line of runoff. "There. Dry enough." She shifted closer to Iris so only she could hear. "Keep her beside you. Something moves that is not a man."

Iris's hands tightened around Cassandra. "What do you mean."

Tala listened to the elder, then chose her own words. "We hunt a hunger that wears skin. It walks when the air turns thin and cold. It leaves marks that match neither hoof nor claw. It eats and is not fed." Her gaze slid toward the dark beyond the huts. "We smelled the metal in the wind before we found your girl."

Earnest heard the elder's next murmur and waited for the English. Tala's tone cooled. "My father says settlers stir the ground and call old things up. He says you will take your shadows away at dawn. Tonight you borrow our fire."

Smoke lowered with the rain and worked along the shelter line. The elder turned from them and gave quiet orders; men pulled the blaze into a tighter bed. Tala stepped back to stand at his side, hands folded over the staff he had leaned against the post. Out past the firelight the marked trunks took on depth, water running in their cuts as if the wood remembered every hand that scored it. Iris drew Cassandra under the eave. Earnest stood a breath longer, lantern still high, as if light alone could keep the village honest. Then he joined them, and the rain drowned the rest.

Chapter 3

Dawn came thin over the riverside village, light pushing through the storm's wreck. Branches hung split and heavy. Needles lay in wet drifts. Mud ribbed the ground and pooled cold at the roots. What embers lived under the wet gave up a sour breath of char.

Earnest stood at the camp's edge with his lantern turned low. The woods beyond held that charged stillness he knew from bad water before a sea rose. Tom's grin flashed and sank. He drew short breaths and said nothing.

Iris tightened Cassandra's blanket under the eave of a cane wall. Her hands moved with a healer's care. Between motions she watched the trees. A metallic tang rode the air. The gouged bark by the river would not leave her thoughts. She crushed a sprig from her pouch; the leaves had gone dark and soft in the rain.

"This land sits wrong," she murmured, and tucked the wool higher.

Cassandra shivered. Mud still rimmed her boots. Sleep had not stayed. "It's out there," she whispered. "I can feel it."

The elder came with staff in hand. Beads clicked once against reed-woven cloth. He spoke to Tala. She listened, then answered in careful English.

"He says feet like yours wake what sleeps. Children of ours have gone. Something hunts when the air thins and turns cold. It wears a body and is never fed."

Earnest faced him. "We have our own roof. We are leaving."

Iris gathered Cassandra. They took the flooded path out of the village. Behind them, Tala watched from the eaves, rainwater pacing off the palmetto in a straight silver line.

Charleston's edge rose through the haze, a steeple stabbing the gray like a crooked finger beckoning them in. Lanes held last night's water. Clapboard roofs sagged. Moss swung low. People moved with lowered voices, glancing toward the timberline as if sound might draw something back.

Along the open market by the river, Gullah boatmen and women stood near their dugouts, baskets of sweetgrass at their feet. Their talk came in the sing-song of the islands, a braid of tongues from across the sea and this coast. They lifted small woven brooms and said they kept a haint from the door. Mothers bartered in quiet tones. A child clung high on a skirt and would not let go.

Closer to the churchyard, the town's work went on at the edges. Enslaved men and women carried water and wood. A woman shouldered a yoke and kept steady over slick ground, lips moving with something like a prayer. A man stacked cord by a sagging porch, hands roughened, wrists scarred pale where iron had bitten years before; the axe met wet wood with a thud that died fast in the damp. An older man walked with two pails that slopped over each step, his frame careful, his eyes fixed on the place he meant to reach. Earnest watched them with the wary look of a sailor reading weather.

At the church door, a tight knot of townsfolk argued in low voices. The talk broke and reshaped as the Yorks drew near.

"It was his doing," a man said, nodding toward the pulpit within. "Says the Lord's house is open to all souls."

"Aye, and now Negroes stand inside like Christians," another muttered.

A woman answered, tired rather than harsh. "At the back, as he set it. Horses still outside. That's the bargain."

"Bargain or no," the first man said, "it turns some stomachs."

Iris took that in and felt something ease toward a pastor she had yet to meet. Earnest gave no sign and pushed the door.

The wooden church crouched under live oaks. Moss trailed like worn cloth. The roof had taken water and bowed. Wind pressed the panes until they rattled. Hinges complained when the door swung. A hymn drifted thin through the crowded room and tangled with the draft.

Stained glass broke gray into red and blue and threw it across the pews. Earnest set his shoulders and sat; the bench gave a small protest and held. Iris laced her fingers to keep them still. Cassandra's blanket had been traded for a dry shawl; the wool scratched and the chill remained. At the rear, Negro men and women stood in a sober row beneath the gallery beam. They kept to their place, heads high, hands quiet. A few Gullah fishers had come in from the market and lined the wall near them, caps in hand. No horses inside, as the door warden half-joked to a latecomer and was met with a frown.

Reverend Collins stood at the pulpit with both hands on a worn Bible. His voice was steady rather than loud.

"As it is written in Psalm thirty-four," he said, "the Lord is nigh unto them that are of a broken heart, and saveth such as be of a contrite spirit." His gaze moved over the room. "Evil often moves in the shade of our own works. The master sowed good seed, and tares rose among it. We will seek His light and root what festers."

Beside him sat his wife. A whisper near the Yorks gave Iris the name when she asked it softly. "Margaret." She was bone-pale beneath the bonnet, breath touched with a small wheeze. Yet a fresh flush colored her cheeks today, an odd brightness after a night like that. Iris's eye, trained by years of tending fever and blood loss, marked the mismatch and said nothing.

"We have lost much," Collins said more quietly, "but He seeks us still. Hold fast."

When the service ended and bodies spilled into the yard, the damp sharpened again. Collins paused at the steps with a woman in a frayed shawl. "Ellie," the yard murmured. A girl gone since last night. He promised to call at the widow's house and turned down the lane.

Margaret crossed to the Yorks with careful steps and a quick, wan smile. "New faces," she said. "I am Margaret, the pastor's wife. I am glad you are here."

"Iris," Iris said. "Earnest. Cassandra."

"We are getting by," Iris added, measuring the woman with a healer's glance and saying nothing of what she saw.

"Town is on edge," Earnest said. "Church does not settle it much."

"We have had a hard run," Margaret answered. Her fingers trembled and stilled. "Children go missing. Long as I remember. Perhaps ten in a year. The Indians say a flesh-eater walks."

"A wendigo," Iris said before she could stop herself.

Margaret's mouth tightened. "I do not set much store by such names," she said. "But the count remains."

A man stepped up with a sure tread. "Jacob," Margaret said. "This is Mr. and Mrs. York, and Cassandra."

"Jacob," he said, offering his hand. Earnest took it. The grip held work and memory.

"Deckhand," Earnest asked, "ever sail into Boston."

"For a spell," Jacob said. "Many times. Do we know each other."

"Twelve winters back," Earnest said. "A greenhorn tangled in rope with the sea turning him upside down."

Jacob smiled. "I hope you learned your knots."

Earnest let out one rough laugh and clasped his shoulder. "I owe you."

"What brings you south," Jacob asked.

"A captain in port offered work," Earnest said. "And I mean to test your whiskey."

"Mr. Collins and I purchased Jacob years ago," Margaret added, quick and breathy. "We freed him. He chose to stay. He keeps wood at my door when the reverend is called out."

Cassandra looked up. "Ellie is the one missing," she asked softly.

Margaret nodded once. "Her mother prays hard."

Earnest's gaze slid toward the trees beyond the yard. "Something is wrong out there," he said. "The river people said their own have vanished."

"They were not warm to us," Jacob said, even and without heat. "Said trouble follows your kind."

Margaret looked back to Cassandra. "You saw a cloak," she said.

"It reached for me," Cassandra answered. "Then a scream came."

"Woods twist sound," Margaret said, voice light, as if to ease the child. "But you are alive, and that is no small thing."

Iris gave a small, careful smile. "Alive and holding," she said. "We will manage."

Wind moved the moss in a long hush. Near the market edge, the island vendors lifted their sweetgrass and sang under their breath. The Negro workers kept to their tasks along the lanes, water sloshing, wood stacked, faces set against the day. A crow called once and went still. Collins turned the corner toward the widow's door, the town closing around its grief like water settling after a wave.

Chapter 4

Tala stood at the river's edge, boots settling into mud as if the bank breathed with an old hunger. The current muttered through the reeds; foam slid out and gathered back. She stilled, listening the way Hassun had taught her as a child: wait long enough and the wild lays its mind bare. A deep beat moved through bone, the same low pulse that had sounded the night Kael slipped under and never rose.

Her fingertips found the bone bead braided into her hair, smooth from years of touch, Kael's last gift tossed with a grin. For your aim, little sister. She dropped to a knee and sifted the bank. Prints hugged the lip. Dry rust edged each step and cracked beneath her nails. Too broad for a man, too tidy for bear, the angles all wrong. She rose, lifted the torch, and let its hiss trace a thin arc over hollows. Shapes skimmed the rim of light and vanished.

Smoke and low voices met her at the village. The longhouse glowed; hides cut with spirals returned the fire in soft loops. Inside, Hassun wore raven feathers across his shoulders. He kept the spiral staff in hand as a sign, not a weapon. Grief had carved him lean, yet his gaze held iron.

"Blood calls a hunger that walks in skin," he said, voice steady. "We do not sit and count graves."

By the hearth, Anah worked a clay bowl. Ash mixed with red under her fingers; a hum moved the room at the level of breath, her chant old as the ridge. Mira, whose boy the river had taken, sat with a bead like Kael's pressed in her palm. "End it," she told Tala, not loud, not pleading, only true.

Hassun set his heel once into the packed clay. "Our fathers moved these flats with open hands. We traded skins for peace. Axes came for the oldest trees, sap on the ground like kin, and a steeple cut our sky. Oaths snapped." His look settled on Tala. "Now the pines stain again. Something wakes when honor breaks."

Anah lifted the bowl. "Hear the rule," she said. "You do not slay the hunger in its skin. Steel, stone, arrow, kill it that way and the wanting slips into the hand that strikes. The old ones learned this at cost. We bind instead, or we cast it where wanting starves." Her eyes flicked to Hassun, then back to Tala. "When we suspect the stain in a soul, we set the proving. Three nights of fasting. Cedar smoke drawn through the mouth. Bone beads laid on the tongue. If the breath turns sweet, if meat draws the eye, we raise the stone circle. Blood answers blood. Cinder balances cinder. The marked are fixed to earth or sent to emptiness, where names thin and drift."

Mira's bead flashed. "My boy felt it by the water," she said. "Little hawk, go."

Promise caught behind Tala's teeth. She gave a single nod and stepped into night.

West of the huts, the torch wrote a narrow road across undergrowth. Nine winters slipped over her as she walked. Kael at her side. His bead dropped into her palm. The two of them reading deer in soft ground while the land hummed its old song. Nothing hides if you listen, he had said. Then a hush that felt wrong. His whisper close. A human cry that snapped and went to silence.

At first light she had found him in a low place, throat opened, beads pale against dark mud. Hassun gathered the scattering with both hands shaking. "We woke a thing when we broke faith," he had said, eyes turned toward the wagons grinding south. Smoke and song sealed the dead. That morning taught the price of vows.

The trail dipped into a sink. Roots laced the floor like veins. At the lip lay a broken arrow fletched with raven feather, her own. The iron head had darkened. The air swelled with rot. She closed her fist until the shaft bit her palm and moved on through cedar where lichen hung like veils. River-sound kept its patient measure.

Another memory rose: her thirteenth winter, a ring of stones under pine, cedar and ash sharp in her nose, Hassun steadying her hands while Anah drew wet spirals on her skin.

We call the ground to answer when a spirit takes on the hunger, Hassun had said. Anah's voice came like gravel over water. We fix the stained to stone, or send the worst where emptiness eats them thin. Rare, Hassun told her. Only the lost. Roan was the last in my time.

A twig gave behind her heel. She stilled. Moss on a nearby trunk brushed back as if a shoulder had slid past.

"Tala," came a whisper.

Lena stepped into the torch glow, hair bound with river shells, forearms streaked with ash. They had tracked side by side since they were small. Lena outran any boy and shot clean to fifty paces. When she spoke, Tala listened. "Anah sent me," she said. "Fresh sign west. Near the stone circle."

Between the pines a thin figure trembled into sight and thinned again, too tall, edges blurred like heat over stone. Tala's bow rose before thought. "Show yourself." Night answered with colder air. Lena let the chant rise, the cadence Anah had beaten into them as girls, a line of notes to steady the hand. Tala loosed. The arrow sang past the blur. A thin sound lifted, high and wrong, like wind forced through a split reed, then tore on the trunks. When the hush returned, a shard of clay sat in the mud, rim stained dark.

She lifted it. A copper taste crept to her tongue and faded. "Roan's ring," Lena said, fingers closing around an arrow at her back. "Or another's. The circle holds, yet something claws."

The shard crumbled in Tala's fist. Prints and shards and a child's blood were not tales. They were tracks.

"If I do not come back," she said, level now, "tell Anah to raise the binding. Use the law."

Lena touched knuckles to the dirt in assent.

They moved. The torch kept a clean edge against the dark. Firs pressed close. Vines trailed like cold fingers over old bark. In her mind the longhouse gathered its circle of bodies and low talk. Hassun's jaw fixed. Anah's bowl waited by the fire. A dull glint near a root drew Tala down. A child's woven cord lay there, fibers stained and frayed. She turned it in her hand. Mira's boy flickered in memory, small hands, a cord like this, then slipped away.

The path fell once more and steadied. The stone circle ahead would be slick with night, set where ground gathers sound and will not return it. Gate or grave, binding or exile. Tala fixed her eyes on the darker run of trees and went.

Chapter 5

Earnest twisted in sleep, hands fisting the blanket as if the cloth were a line slipping through tarred palms. A low sound climbed his throat and stopped. The room dimmed to a seam of gray and then fell away.

Lantern smoke flattened beneath a lath of beam. Wet wool, old pitch, and close breath soured the hall. Bodies pressed in, a swell of elbows and mutters. Iron cuffs scored half-moons into his wrists. The magistrate held Earnest's whalebone charm between two fingers, the carving dulled by salt and years.

"Witch's mark," the man cried, and struck the bench. Dust leapt from the grain. A fisherman spat that nets had rotted and fields gone sour. From the rear a woman screamed to burn him.

Iris sat near the front, heavy with their second child. Boots shoved past, grinding herbs spilled from her pouch into the boards. She stood like a mast that refuses to bow. "I heal," she said, clear through heat and stink. "Judge that." The hall tightened around her words. Pride and fear braided together inside Earnest until the pull split skin beneath iron.

"Craft, not curses," he told them, turning his voice to cut and pull. "Your knots fail because your hands do." Stones answered. The magistrate named exile or fire. A torch swung too close and heat licked his cheek. A guard Earnest had paid in a quiet tavern weeks earlier slid near, slipped a key into the lock, and let the chain drop.

"Go," the man breathed.

Earnest shouldered toward Iris. "We are leaving," he rasped to his wife. He took her arm, steadied her weight, and forced a path toward the door. Cold air hit like a blade dipped in water. Iris faltered. A sound tore loose from her and bent him at the ribs. Blood spread across her skirt in a quick, dark bloom.

They did not flee without Cassandra. The girl had been laid down at Mrs. Pike's two doors over when the shouting began. Earnest cut down the alley, lifted the sleeping child, and brought her back before the street turned ugly. By the time the horse took the road, Cassandra lay between them, warm from sleep, cheek tucked under Iris's palm.

Frost silvered the ruts. Reins rasped his palms until they ran. Wind clawed the words from Iris's mouth, yet her tone held steady. "We will outrun it." At first light they turned into a shallow vale and stopped. He ripped cloth from his coat, bound her hands, and held them until the shaking eased. The horse steamed in the cold and stood patient.

"No more running," he said.

"No more burning," she answered. They set the vow between them and kept it like banked fire on a long night.

The road south took days. They slept in hollows and by cutbanks, roused to owls and fox bark. In the dark hours, he woke to her fingers finding his, both of them listening to the wind comb fields they would never see again. He learned the weight of silence that follows a name left behind. He learned the way a small child sighs in sleep when a wagon wheel finds a smoother line. By the time the marshes began and the river smell took hold of the air, Danvers had thinned to a set of sounds he carried like old scars.

Earnest surfaced hard. Board seams bled a pale strip of morning. Frost feathered the window corners. The hearth held two sullen coals.

"It is past," Iris said, already awake. Her hand found his forearm and steadied the breaths that wanted to race.

By the fire, Cassandra pushed upright under her shawl. "It is here," she said. "I heard it again. Reaching, like before." She kept her eyes on the door as if patience alone might make the thing name itself.

Iris sat and kept her palm on Earnest's shoulder. "Same dream," she asked, eyes on him.

"The crowd," he said. "The dock. Iron." He let the rest stay under.

Cassandra's voice drew tight. "You did not hear me. It is here."

"I hear you," Iris answered at once. She swung her legs to the floor and pressed warmth into her feet with both hands. "We meet it with light, not guesswork."

Earnest set his soles on the cold boards and stood. "We heard you," he told Cassandra, plain and direct. His fingers brushed the whalebone handle at his belt because habit asked for it, not because steel had ever settled a haunting. He crossed to the window, scraped a cloud from the frost with his thumb, and peered through. The yard lay pewter and still. The fence ran a wan line to the trees.

Iris fed a split stick to the coals. The small flame climbed, stuttering, then held. "We keep to sense," she said. "Enough light to see clean, then we look."

He lifted the latch. Cold edged around his knees. Pine and river mud rode the air, a thin warning along the teeth. He stepped onto the stoop. Frost crisped under his boots. Iris came to his shoulder. Cassandra slipped between them and gripped the top rail of the fence, knuckles chalk-white on the gray wood.

A figure stood by the far post. Taller than a man yet frail at the edges, as if cut from breath. It lifted a hand. Fingers curled inward, trembling with a jerky will. The place where eyes should hold light showed only depth. The mouth worked without sound. For a blink the posture pleaded. Then the shape thinned and slid into the pines. The rail gave one dry note and went still.

Cassandra's nails marked the wood. "You saw," she whispered.

“I saw,” Iris said. She gauged the distance the way a midwife reads a laboring body, by what can be borne and what must be braced.

Earnest let the knife rest in its sheath. “We hold the door,” he said. “We wait for the sun to climb. Then we choose our move.”

They did not turn away at once. The three of them stood with shoulders almost touching, watching the place where the fence met the trees. The yard shifted by degrees from iron to pewter to dull silver. A crow gave a single call and fell silent. Water ticked in the eaves. When light laid a clean line along the rail, they stepped back inside and set the latch.

Iris brought the kettle from the coals and poured what the fire would give. Steam scrolled into the room and faded. Cassandra wrapped her shawl tighter, then lowered it from her mouth and spoke low. “It is the same reach,” she said. “The river night and this one. The hand curls the same.”

Earnest pulled a chair nearer the hearth and sat where he could face both door and window. “Tell it plain,” he said, not unkindly. “From waking, not from fear.”

Cassandra nodded, gathered herself, and laid the moments in a row. The river. The reaching. The word that sounded like no and carried a plea. The sprint through dark trunks. The plunge. The rough hands that hauled her from the current. The night in the village, fire and rain. As she spoke, the room seemed to lean closer, boards ticking as frost let go of nail heads.

Iris listened with her healer's stillness, hands quiet on her knees. When the girl finished, she spoke as if naming a fever. "It shows itself only when night sits heavy. It does not cross the fence. It reaches. It does not take." Her gaze slid to Earnest. "That reads like a boundary."

"Or a trick," he answered, but there was less bite than before. He looked again at the door and the thin wedge of light that gathered at its foot. "We wait for the sun to be honest. Then we walk the line from post to post and learn what we can."

"Together," Iris said.

"Together," he agreed.

Cassandra lifted her chin. "I am coming," she said.

"You will be between us," Iris answered, and that was settled.

They ate the last heel of bread with a little broth and fastened their coats. The day had taken firmer hold by the time they stepped out again. Smoke rose from two distant roofs. A dog barked once and gave up. The trees beyond the fence stood with their winter look, each needle a small length of glass, each length catching light like filings in a bowl.

At the far post, Earnest crouched and studied the rime on the rail. A track lay on the yard side where frost had softened and then skinned over again. No boot tread. No hoof. A shape like fingers, yet longer, pressed once and gone.

They traced the fence line to the corner and back. The same single mark appeared twice more, set at the height of a reaching arm. The trees offered nothing but three small slivers of bark on the inner side, as if a body had slid past and taken a shaving with it. When they turned for the house, the yard looked no different than it had at dawn, and yet the place felt newly measured, a room where furniture had shifted while no one watched.

Inside, Earnest hung the knife back on its peg. "We will speak to Collins," he said. "And to Jacob." He did not say the other thought, the thought of Tala's warning by the riverbank. Iris said it for him.

"We will send word up the path to the village," she said. "Courtesy, if nothing else."

Cassandra drew nearer the fire and held out her hands. "It will come again," she said, not afraid now, only certain.

"Then it will meet us in our right minds," Iris answered. She laid a palm to the girl's hair and left it there, steady as a hand on a helm.

Outside, the light climbed the fence and tipped into the trees. The house breathed as the day warmed a finger's width. Somewhere down by the river, ice let go of a root and turned in the slow water. The three of them sat and listened, each holding a different silence, and the small flame held its line.

Chapter 6

Earnest set a round on the block and brought the axe down. The haft jarred in his palms. Chips jumped and skittered across the dirt. Work would have to hold the line after the thing at the fence.

"Stack close to the wall," he said.

Cassandra hauled a limb toward the growing pile by the house. Bark bit her palms. "Heavy," she said, but she kept moving.

Iris knelt at the kindling, twigs breaking clean in her hands. She glanced once at the trees, then back to the work, quick and precise, like someone counting a pulse.

Earnest lifted again. The axe caught a buried knot and kicked. Shock ran up his arm. His boots slid on a slick patch of moss. The head tore free and swung low. Iron grazed his shin. Cloth parted. Heat flared and ran. He dropped the axe and swore. Blood darkened his trouser and dotted the ground.

Iris was up in an instant. "Hold still." She pressed above the cut, tore a strip from her skirt, and bound it tight with quick turns. "Cass, water."

Cassandra sprinted to the bucket by the porch and brought it back half-sloshed. Iris rinsed the wound. Pink curled through the runoff, then cleared. The gash was ugly but clean. She tied the cloth firm and met his eyes.

"You will favor it a few days," she said. "Sit when I tell you."

He gave a short nod. "Seen worse at sea."

She wiped her hands on her hem, then lifted her head. The air beyond the yard carried a sour note, like meat kept too long. She filed it away.

Footsteps came from the trees. Earnest eased his knife from his belt and shifted his weight to the good leg. Lantern light moved between the trunks, and Reverend Collins stepped into the clearing.

"York," Collins called. "Heard you were settled. Thought to look in." His gaze took in the bandage at Earnest's shin, the knife, then returned to their faces.

"What for," Earnest said. "We manage."

The reverend raised a small bundle wrapped in linen. Rust-colored patches bled through the weave. He loosened the knot and showed what lay inside: a bone bead, carved with a shallow spiral, stained dark. The cord was frayed and tacky.

"I found this near the bend," Collins said. "Beside prints. A boy is missing. Matthew's youngest."

Iris stepped forward. "When."

"Last night," he said. "The blood was fresh when I reached it. Small feet in a hurry. No man's step beside them."

Cassandra set the bucket down and moved to Iris's side. "It is the same as before," she said. "By the river. By our fence. It reached. Then it cried out."

Collins looked at her, then back to Earnest. "You spoke of a figure earlier. I am not here to start a gallows. I want a clear account."

Earnest kept the knife low. "We did not put that bead there. We touched no child. We saw a cloak move along the bank and heard a cry. That is what happened."

He studied the bead again. The spiral matched cuts he had seen on trunks near the village, and the stain said the town would start pointing — first at the tribes, then at strangers. "Where exactly," he asked. "Which bend."

"Downstream of the old ferry stump," Collins said. He wrapped the bead again, slower this time, as if it might leave a mark. "The talk has begun. Some blame the tribes. Some blame newcomers. I would rather have facts than fires."

"Then ask at the river," Earnest said. "Ask the people who pulled our girl from it. They watch that water like kin."

Collins weighed him, then nodded. "I will speak to them. And to Matthew. He keeps a shack near that bend. Quiet man. Too much loss can turn quiet wrong."

"Speak to him yourself," Iris said. "Do not let a crowd do it for you."

Collins's eyes shifted once toward the trees. "I aim to. The wind has teeth tonight." He tucked the linen away. "Bar your door by dark. If you learn more, bring it to me. I will listen."

Cassandra stepped forward. "I am the one it chased. It is not my father. It is not us."

Collins held her gaze. "I heard you." He lifted the lantern and turned back to the pines. The glow thinned and went out among the trunks.

Silence pooled. A jay scolded once and stopped. Far off, the river kept its low talk.

Iris looked to the fence line, then to Earnest's leg. "Sit," she said, softer now. "I will change the cloth once more."

He lowered himself to the stump and set the knife across his thigh. Cassandra brought the axe to the wall and leaned it careful of the edge.

"We go to the bend at first light," Earnest said. "Then to Collins. Then we send word up the path to Tala."

"Together," Iris answered.

Cassandra nodded. "Between you," she said.

"That is the way," Iris told her.

They stacked the last of the wood and carried it inside. Warmth rose slow from the hearth. Iris cleaned the cut and tied a fresh band. Earnest watched door and window both. Cassandra sat with her shawl around her shoulders and the bead's shape fixed in her mind, white in lantern light, like a tooth set on cloth.

Evening took the yard. They ate what there was. Before the latch went down, the three of them stood at the threshold and marked the fence, the trees, the slice of sky above the clearing. Nothing moved. Still, the place felt newly measured, as if a hand had run along every board while their backs were turned.

"Sun, then river," Iris said.

"Sun, then river," Earnest echoed.

They set the bar and let the house hold. Outside, the light faded to ash, and the river kept its steady note.

Chapter 7

Reverend Collins trudged through the mire, cloak heavy with damp, lantern held low so its light stayed tight to the ground. Each step worked a dull thud from the path. He kept his eyes ahead, past the last fence and into the lean dark where the widow lived alone.

The shack leaned at the settlement's edge, a crooked thing patched with warped planks. Wind worried the seams and made a thin whistle through every gap. The roof had taken moss and kept it. Stones in the yard showed frost-split faces. A small shoe lay tipped near the sill. Beside it, a wooden horse stared with one chipped eye.

"Mary," he called, and knocked.

She opened slow. Her shawl hung in strings; the rosary in her hand clicked once. "Reverend."

"May I."

She stepped back. The room smelled of stale wax and wet straw. Ash lay thick in the hearth, a dull gray that swallowed light. Near the threshold, a dark-stained scrap sat where she had placed it. A tin cup on its side had dried to a pale ring. A child's doll slumped near the leg of a stool, button mouth askew.

"I found the cloth by morning," Mary said. "Right at the door." Her voice shook, then steadied with effort. "He said he heard something call. I caught his sleeve — but he slipped away. The door flew open, and the night took him. By the time the rain cleared, all I could see was the shoe... and that."

Collins crouched, lifted the cloth with two fingers. The iron smell rose and stayed. He folded it, careful, and tucked it inside his cloak.

"The Lord is near to the broken," he said, and though the words were true, their comfort felt thin in the small room. "You did what a mother can do."

Mary's hand hushed the rosary for a breath. "If you find him walking," she said, "bring him through this door yourself. If he is not... tell me plain."

"I will tell you plain," he said.

A shape filled the doorway behind him. A young woman stood there with mud to her boots, bow at her back, palm raised.

"Tala," she said. "Hassun's daughter." Her gaze took in Mary and then fixed on Collins. "We have a boy gone."

"Come in," Collins said.

She stepped onto the boards and kept to one side of the lantern's circle. "My cousin, Kael. Two nights ago at the bend. We found beads in mud and curves in blood. No tracks away." She tapped the pouch at her belt. "Your nights line with ours."

"They do," Collins said. He turned to Mary. "You are not alone in this."

Mary nodded once, and her eyes shone.

Tala studied Collins. "I ask you direct, preacher — has anyone grown strong when these losses come? A face that lifts as the rest of you bow."

He thought of Margaret's poor color and the strange mornings when, after a night of wailing, her hand steadied on the cup and her step held better. He did not shape the thought into accusation. "My wife is sick," he said. "On some mornings after hard nights, she manages more. I have no tidy name for that."

"Our elders say hunger can bind itself to a person and pull from others," Tala said. "When it feeds, the one it favors rises." She drew a careful breath. "Another thing. You do not end a wendigo with a blade. If you strike it down, the hunger sets its teeth in you. We bind or starve, but we do not 'kill' and walk away clean."

"How do you bind," Collins asked, "if it comes to that."

"Circle. Chant. The right place, the right moon. Blood is named and made powerless. We keep that rite for the truly marked." Her jaw set. "I would rather catch the living hand that feeds it."

Mary's fingers worked the beads again, faster than before.

The wind pressed at the door. The lantern shook once. Outside, something shifted against the yard's edge — a quiet rearranging of shadow. Collins lifted the light and stepped to the threshold.

A figure stood by the fence, thin and too tall, cloak drooping from narrow shoulders. It raised one hand. Fingers curled and shook. Where eyes should have held a glint there was only depth. The mouth moved without voice. The posture — pleading — lasted a heartbeat, then the shape turned sidewise and thinned into the line of pines. The wooden horse knocked softly where it swung.

Tala was already at Collins's shoulder, knife low. "That shape walked our tree line last night," she said. "Twice."

Collins held the lantern steady. "It showed at the Yorks' fence at first light," he said. "Reached for the girl and went to shadow when we moved toward it."

They stepped out together. The mud along the fence had taken a single press where fingers might have rested, then skinned over. Tala crouched and ran two fingers along the damp. She lifted a bead from the churn — bone, carved, its tie frayed and stained. She let it fall back.

"Someone lays these to send blame," she said. "The hand is the thing. Not the token."

Collins moved the lantern slow along the yard. A sliver of stained cloth showed where the fence rail met a post, caught on a splinter and now stiff. He pried it free. "Same weave as yours," he told Mary, "but not the same color. I will take this, too."

Mary's grip tightened on the rosary. "Bring me my boy if he walks," she said again. "If not, speak truth."

"I will," Collins said. He looked to Tala. "At first light, the bend. There is a shack west of here that sits in my thoughts. Meet me there, and bring the mark of any circles you know to look for."

Tala gave a single nod. "Dawn."

"Lock your door, Mary," Collins said. "Keep a flame. If he comes home, do not let him out again in the dark." He touched her shoulder like a blessing, though the weight in his own chest did not ease.

When he and Tala stepped into the yard, the night closed quick and clean. The figure did not show again. Tala melted toward the trees and was gone, moving like she had left pieces of herself in the dark to guide her back.

Collins stood with the lantern near his thigh, the flame a small, stubborn eye. He set his jaw on a prayer with no ornament and started back through the lanes.

Halfway to town, he cut across to the church. The door was barred; he had barred it himself. He let himself in and climbed to the gallery. From there, he could see the back row where Negroes stood on Sundays — his doing, his line in the dust, the one right choice he knew with certainty. He rested both hands on the rail and let the emptiness listen.

He spoke under his breath to the quiet room. "Grant me sight to know my own house. Grant me mercy enough to hold a truth that will break it."

When he left the church, the lantern showed a pale seam along the east where morning would come. He kept it in front of him and walked for the river.

Chapter 8

The Collins home crouched at the town's rim. One candle troubled the dark. Margaret sat at the table with both hands around a tin cup and kept her eyes on the door latch, as if patience alone might hold it closed.

The latch clicked.

Jacob stepped inside with river mud on his coat. He shut the door with his heel and set a clay bowl on the table. The liquid rocked once and slicked to the rim.

The smell reached her first. Margaret flinched and drew her hands back. "Please," she said, and the word rasped. "Not tonight."

"It keeps you standing." Jacob's voice was rough and sure. He slid the bowl toward her. "Drink."

Her breath came shallow and uneven. The candle made a small halo on her cheek and showed how near the bone sat in her face. "It isn't right."

"It keeps you breathing," he said again, as if that were the only measure that mattered. His wrists shifted, and old scars flashed pale at the cuff. He watched her like a man waiting for an order to be obeyed.

"Whose," she asked, not lifting her eyes from the bowl.

He did not answer. The corner of his mouth moved.

She touched the rim with two fingers and pulled them back as if the clay had burned. "If I drink," she said, voice thin but earnest, "you stop leaving trinkets where children play. No beads set in mud. No talk that poisons a healer's name."

"You keep to your end. I keep to mine," he said. He tapped the pouch at his belt and let the beads knock together once, quiet and certain. "There's talk. York saw light where light should not be. The preacher's asking after it. Best I stack the ground before the sun's up."

"They share bread," she said, and she hated that her voice shook. "They are not the kind who stir harm."

"They stir suspicion by standing where they stand," he said. "Drink."

The bowl felt heavier than the table. Margaret raised it a finger's width, set it down, then raised it again because the tremor would not stop on its own. She took a mouthful, gagged once, and forced it down. Warmth moved through her in a way that both eased and shamed. She took another, smaller, and set the bowl down hard enough that it rang.

Her breath steadied. She hated the relief for how fast it came.

Jacob wiped the edge with his thumb, left a smear on the wood, and paced a short line between door and hearth. "When you wake tomorrow, you'll feel the floor under you," he said. "That is the only sermon I carry."

"I will not wake clean," she said. "And neither will you."

He shrugged as if that were a small matter. "Clean does not keep a body alive."

"It keeps a soul from rotting," she said, almost under her breath.

He stopped at the door. "I have work."

"What work," she asked, though she knew. The question bought a few seconds of him not walking away.

"Work you cannot pull me from," he said, hand already on the latch.

"Then I will warn the ones you aim to cut," she said, surprising herself. "I will go to Iris York. To the preacher. To anyone who will listen."

"Go," he said. "Tell the town your husband's wife lives by a bowl." His face did not gloat; it tightened. "See where that leaves you, and him."

He stepped out, and the house took the silence back. The candle narrowed. Margaret stared at her hands as if they belonged to some other woman who had chosen wrong and kept on choosing it.

She stood and crossed to the little cross on the wall. It hung crooked where a dozen evenings of prayer had set it askew. She set her palm flat to it to feel something fixed and cold.

"Forgive me," she said. No further words came.

She wiped the table clean with a rag, once, twice, until the wood shone where it had been stained. The smell still lingered, but the gleaming wood made the room feel orderly, if only for a moment. She folded the rag and set it by the basin.

On the shelf near the door lay the small Bible Collins had given her when fever first laid her low. Between two pages, she kept a scrap for notes to herself. She pulled it free and, with a stub of charcoal, wrote four words in a hand that shook: Do not trust beads. She folded the slip and tucked it in her sleeve.

The room had its own small sounds. The cross ticked against the nail when the draft found it. A mouse skittered and then thought better of it. Far off, a cart wheel clicked on its weak spoke. A dog barked once and did not bother again.

She thought of Collins's hand steadying hers at vespers, and how that steadiness had held for the space of one breath. She thought of the York girl's bright, frightened eyes at the church and the way the mother had stood half a step forward — enough to meet a blow, not enough to start a fight. She did not know their past; she only knew what she had seen.

She poured water into a cup and drank because something cleaner needed to wash her mouth. When she set the cup down, the bowl's shadow still cut the table in two. She turned the bowl over and left it that way.

A thin resolve took shape where dread had sat. In the morning, she would walk to the preacher's door and put the folded note in his hand. If he asked how she knew, she would say, I listen. If he pressed, she would say, I am done being quiet.

She banked the candle and moved to the pallet. Lying on her side, she kept her face turned to the faint seam of light at the shutter. Sleep did not take her. The body rested because there was nothing else it could do.

Far off, the river kept its constant voice. If she had listened for words, she might have said it named her and then named her again, softer. She did not listen for that. She counted her breaths and held the next one when she reached ten. Then she started over.

Toward dawn, the floorboards cooled underfoot. She rose and dressed. The note made a small weight against her wrist where she had tied it under her sleeve.

Down by the bend, a shack drew the first color from the coming day. Collins would be there with his lantern. Somewhere in the trees, Tala would already be counting the steps between prints. Margaret lifted the latch and stepped into the lane.

The air tasted of woodsmoke and river. She turned toward the church. Behind her, the house closed on its hinge and said nothing about what had happened inside it. She did not look back.

At the corner, Jacob's track ran west. She kept to the other side of the ruts and walked faster.

Chapter 9

A scrape along the yard rail woke Cassandra.

She sat up fast. The hearth had gone to a low red, and the room held a thin chill that lived in the seams between boards. The house breathed in its old way. One board sighed. A rafter ticked. Then the scrape came again, small and deliberate, as if a hand tested the fence.

"Father?" she whispered.

Earnest shifted and settled. His bandaged shin had bled through the cloth; the dark patch showed in the ember's little light. Iris's arm lay across the quilt, palm open, fingers slack. No answer from either of them. Only the faint rasp of sleep and the hush after it.

Cassandra crossed to the window. Frost had laced the pane. She rubbed a circle clear with the heel of her hand and peered out. The yard was a shallow dish of gray. The top rail showed a thin rim of pale. Between the fence posts the trees made a darker band and, there, something stood where the rail turned. Tall and still. The shape looked like a cutout in the night. A slow bend of the head. A lift of one arm, the movement stiff, like a joint long unused.

Glass and frost swallowed sound. She made no more of it through the pane than the weight of its watching and the way the air seemed to hold itself.

She turned the latch.

Cold slid inside along the floor. She stepped onto the stoop because she wanted the truth of distance. How far it stood. Whether it had crossed the fence line. Whether it came on. The old fear rose in her throat and met something harder. Whatever pressed at their borders had come twice now. Better to read it plain than to dream it worse.

The night smelled of sap and damp wood. Mud had glazed hard with frost. She kept one hand on the post and leaned enough to look. The figure did not move. It faced the house. No wind troubled the pines, yet the edge of its cloak fretted as if in a draft of its own making. When it tilted, the hood slipped to a ragged angle and showed a sliver of face. Cheek bone. A wet track on skin. A mouth opening once without sound.

"Who are you," she said, not loud.

The head turned a fraction, as if the question tugged a cord. The hand lifted and closed, not in threat but in a reach she felt low in the body. For a breath the posture held, a mute petition, and then the shape thinned where it met the dark. It slid along the fence and fell back into the trees.

Behind her, the bed ropes creaked. Earnest had found his knife.

"What's out there, girl?" he said, voice rough with sleep.

She kept her eyes on the place where the figure had stood. "The same as by the river. At the corner post. It watched. It reached. Then it turned west."

Iris came to the door, hair loose, shawl gripped tight. "Did it cross?" she asked.

"No," Cassandra said. "It kept to the far side of the rail."

Iris's gaze went to the corner. "A boundary," she said, as to herself. "Or the fear of one."

Earnest stepped onto the stoop, tested his leg, and held the post with his free hand. "We are not chasing it blind," he said. "We wait for a clean light and follow sign from post to post."

"Together," Iris said.

"Together," he answered.

They stood until the cold made their cheeks ache. Nothing moved at the tree line. No voices carried. Only the soft tick of frost letting go of the eaves. When the quiet felt honest again, they barred the door.

Cassandra crouched by the hearth while Iris coaxed flame from a single stick. The little fire took and held. Earnest eased into the chair where he could see both door and window and unwound the stained strip from his shin. Iris looked once, then twice, and fetched clean cloth and a bowl.

"Tell it from waking," she said to Cassandra, "not from fright."

So Cassandra laid the moments in order. The scrape. The pane. The shape at the corner. The reach. The turn toward the river's bend. She did not add more. She did not claim what she could not have seen or heard through glass.

"It waits and it chooses," Iris said when the girl was done. "It does not come in."

Earnest washed the cut with steady hands. He had a sailor's habit for simple work. Rinse. Press. Bind. The cloth drew a lighter stain this time. "Fence at first light," he said. "If there is sign, we read it. If not, we speak with Collins and with Tala both."

"Collins means for the shack at dawn," Iris said. "He will be west."

"Then we all come to the same ground," Earnest said, and left it there.

The house settled. Heat climbed a finger's breadth from the hearth. Iris laid a small line of ashes across the sill and the inner lintel, a habit learned in sickrooms where she had kept order against fever and fear. Not a charm. A mark to show in the morning if any draft had shifted more than plain weather. She set a cup of water on the table and looked to Cassandra. "Drink," she said. "Then sit with your shawl and rest your eyes. Dawn reads better when the body has a little strength."

Cassandra drank and did as she was told. The picture that rose as she drifted was not Danvers with torches and ropes. It was the corner post in gray light. A palm print on rime. The faint scuff where a sleeve brushed wood. Reading the world in marks steadied her more than any speech could.

They woke to a thin wash of pale. They did not speak in the first minutes. Earnest pulled on his coat. Iris wrapped a scarf. Cassandra pinned her shawl. They stepped out together.

Frost still held in the shaded places. At the corner, a chain of faint ovals ran along the far side of the rail where something had leaned or braced. Longer than a hand. Not hoof. Not boot. On the yard side, undisturbed rime. A single thread of dark fiber snagged in a splinter at the top rail, the kind a rough cloak leaves behind. Halfway down the post, a smear the size of a thumb where resin had lifted from the grain and then dulled, as if a sleeve had taken the shine.

Earnest touched the fiber to his lip the way men test a line for grit. It felt like nothing. He folded it into his palm and pocketed it. "Mark it," he said.

Iris took a bit of charcoal from her pouch and drew a small cross on the inside face of the post. Not prayer. A surveyor's habit. "If it moves again," she said, "we will know where it favors."

"Step clear," Cassandra said. She crouched and looked along the lower rail where frost thinned. In two places it had sunk and skinned over again, the kind of sag that happens when weight brushes light. Each spot stood at the height of a grasping arm. Each faced the house.

They followed the fence to the back corner. There the grass lay pressed in a narrow run toward the trees, as if a body had learned that path by use. No bead. No curled sign in the mud. Only the color of the ground, a shade darker between two pines and then lost among needles.

Earnest stood with his hands on the top rail and looked west. "It keeps the line," he said. "It watches. It goes."

"Then we choose when to meet it," Iris said. "Not the other way."

He nodded. "We take the road. Slow. Eyes low first, then wide."

They walked the outer path that skirted the yard. Iris kept a hand on Cassandra's shoulder when the ground dipped. Earnest paused now and again to look for a broken twig or a lifted chip of bark. Once he found a shallow scrape in the outer face of a post where the grain had roughened. His thumbnail caught there. He left it and moved on.

When the trees took them, the light broke into pieces on needles and old cones. A jay scolded once and fell off. The river's sound lay out ahead like a drawn line. The track they had seen from the yard ran toward it and then leaned to higher ground. Where the rise began, Iris stopped them with a glance.

"Listen," she said.

They did. No footfall. No voice. Only the even rush of water and the small creak of a limb in a light stir. She picked a twig from the path and held it across at knee height. The twig cleared the track for ten strides and then would have struck a shin. That is where she found what she wanted. A faint brush along a stalk of dead grass, cut clean, not by teeth but by speed.

"Tall," she said. "Or longer in the arm than us."

Earnest looked to the river again. "We do not step into the bend alone," he said. "We hold to the oak above it and wait for

Collins if he has sense. If he does not, we walk down in a line and on our feet, not crouched. If it watches, it may mind that."

They reached the oak and set themselves where the roots made a kind of bench. From there they could see the swale and the path down. The shack lay still out of sight, but the light that used to glow from its seams had gone with the night. Smoke rose thin from two roofs back toward town. An owl whoed. The day made its slow work of turning frost to wet at the edges.

Cassandra watched the place where their track opened to the last stand of trees above the water. She wanted to speak and did not. Iris looked at her face and spoke instead.

"When it reached, what did you feel," she asked. "Not fear. The other thing."

"Like a pull that is not mine," Cassandra said after a moment. "Like I owed it something and had forgotten to pay."

Iris inclined her head. "Names have weight," she said. "Promises too. Tala's people bind a hunger by calling it what it is and by telling the truth about debt. We have truth. We will use it."

Earnest had said little. He pressed a palm to his bandage once and let his hand fall. "We keep sense," he said. "We keep together. We keep daylight."

Cassandra drew the shawl closer and sat straighter on the oak root. The picture that rose for her now was not the hood pulled low at the fence. It was a palm print in thawing frost and a line in the grass where feet had gone often. It was a place to stand that gave a clean view of the bend and of any man or thing that came up from it.

A jay spoke again, closer this time. The river lifted a little with wind from the east. Earnest shifted to ease his leg. Iris laid two small stones on the root near her knee in a straight line, then a third to mark the hour when the light reached them. It was an old habit from long watches. It turned waiting into work.

"Collins will come," she said without looking up. "Or Tala will. Either way, we meet them here."

"And if neither," Earnest said.

"Then we will have the ground measured," Iris answered, "and we will be the ones who tell it plain."

They settled to the stillness. The day's first insects woke under the leaf mold. A thread of steam rose from a patch where the sun found the dark soil. The oak's shadow shortened a hand's width. On the far bank, a heron lifted from a sand bar and slid downstream, slow and sure.

"Father," Cassandra said, not taking her eyes from the path, "when you first sailed, how did you learn to read a storm before you felt it."

"You taste the air and you trust the small signs," he said. "A line on the water. A quiet where it should chatter. A gull dropping lower than its habit. You do not ask it to be thunder before you believe it is weather."

Cassandra nodded once. "This is weather," she said.

"Aye," Earnest said. "And we have taken worse by choice or by luck."

They waited. When the sun climbed enough to lay a bright strip along the path, the three stones said a little time had passed. Iris brushed them aside and set them again. Out beyond, a figure moved among the pines. Lantern light dipped once and steadied. The shape came on with a human gait and a measured care.

"Collins," Earnest said.

"Good," Iris said. "We speak with our mouths and with what we have read. Not with fear."

Cassandra kept her eyes on the opening and rose only when the pastor raised his hand to show he had seen them. She felt the pull in her belly ease a point, as if work had been named and time had been given edges. Whatever waited at the bend had watched their fence and kept its side of it. Now they would keep theirs, and walk down together when the ground and the light were ready.

Chapter 10

Jacob kept the torch hooded with his palm and slipped down the cutbank to the pocket of earth he'd chosen at dusk. Two roots crossed like ribs; the ground held. He worked by habit: vial under the narrow flame, rope eased aside, hands steady. When the vial warmed he capped it, fast and clean, and pressed spirals into the wet soil with the knife tip — a tight curl he always used. Not the long, ragged rakes he'd seen gouged into bark upriver. Those belonged to a different story. He let that story do some of his labor.

The forest choked on its own breath where frost pooled low. Wind slid past the crowns with barely a sound; water talked to stone beyond the reeds. He covered what must not be found and stood. No prayer. No pause. He checked his tools, his sleeves, the ground behind him for shine.

On the way out he stopped at a cedar with four deep scars. He set his blade in one groove to measure. Wider than steel, rough-edged. Tala had a name for it that he did not say aloud. He preferred names that answered to his hands.

East of the bend, the churchyard climbed out of river fog. Jacob crushed a pinch of yarrow and sage he had lifted from Iris York's garden and dusted the black mud where the girl's throat had opened earlier that night. The scent was sharp enough to sting his eyes. He brushed the last crumbs into the seam of a boot print and stepped back. Collins liked patterns. Jacob would give him one.

A latch scraped in the lane. He kept to the hedge. "Herbs by the stain," he told the shadowed doorway, voice low and hoarse. "Iris York's work. Tell the reverend." A pale hand clutched shawl to throat. The door shut. The message would walk on its own.

He turned north and cut into the trees. Tala's passage showed in the soft ground: a compact tread and a scuff where a fletching had brushed a stone. Two nights ago her arrow had slipped his sleeve and burned a line along his arm. Close enough to sting. Never again.

From his pocket he took a small plait — Thomas Hale's wrist-cord, cut the night the boy ran to the river. He laid it where his path eased toward the shack, ten paces off the main track. Far enough to make a careful tracker step aside. Near enough that no tracker would miss it.

The shack breathed dull red between river birch. Margaret sat at the table with cloth and steel, working an edge she'd already cleaned twice. Her hands were steadier than in spring; she had made them steady.

"Another," she said, not looking up.

"For us," Jacob answered. He set the sealed vial beneath the table lip and wiped the knife. "By noon there will be talk about Iris. Agree when you are asked. Do not add."

"She gave me tea when fever took me," Margaret said. "She is not our enemy."

"She will be if we do not choose her first." He slid the stolen herb pouch to the shelf with twine and rags. "Collins watches you. Better he watch her."

Margaret sat back. Her breath rasped and caught, then leveled. "The marks on the trees," she whispered. "Those long ones. Tala says that is not your work. She spoke a rule at the fire. If you kill it, it takes you. They bind the ones they suspect and send them out under moons until the hunger breaks."

Jacob set the blade flat on the table. "I do not plan to test their rules. I steer men at men." He tipped his head at the door. "Rest. I'll sit a while."

She gathered the cloths because her fingers needed a task. "Blood for blood," she said, voice thin and automatic, then caught herself and swallowed the phrase. "We keep breathing," she finished instead.

He left her with the lamp and stepped out. The shack's ember faded behind him. Downriver, the tide turned and the current thickened; tonight it hummed like a wire drawn tight. He moved with it, torch low.

A person stood just at the lip of his light. For a breath he thought of the pale figure that haunted the York fence, the one that raised a shaking hand and made no sound. This shape carried a bow. Tala stepped forward, a strip of linen tied above her elbow where something had grazed.

"Your handle," she said, eyes on the whalebone. "I have seen another like it."

"Many sailors carve whale bone," Jacob said. "Good grip in rain."

She did not bother with his face. She watched his boots, then looked past him at the shack's faint glow. "There are curls cut into wet earth west of here. Not claws. A hand that likes its work."

"Your stories say claws," he said.

"My elders say claws," she answered. "My eyes say hand." She nodded toward the trail. "You placed a child's cord where I would find it. I found it. Do not pretend you are not leading me."

He weighed the knife and left it on the table in his mind. An arrow travels faster than a step. He kept his hands still. "You came alone."

"Not for long," she said. "My kin walk behind me. A preacher with a lamp walks behind them. He knows a rule now." She took him in, unblinking. "You cannot kill a wendigo without wearing it. There is a rite for those marked — to bind or to throw beyond us. If Collins finds the wrong thing first, a woman burns."

"Then guide him," Jacob said. "You know the woods."

"I guide my own," she said. "If I see proof." Her gaze ticked to the dark smear at his cuff where fern had brushed damp into the cloth. She didn't step closer. "I will bring him to claw marks and not to curls. If I find curls, I bring him to a door."

"Bring who you like," Jacob said. "Doors hold."

"Not here," she said, and she was gone between trunks, as quiet as the shadow of a hawk.

He waited until the torch was a thumb of light. Tala would pace and count and listen for the way his footfalls struck roots; he gave her nothing. He slid down to the creek stone and walked in water until the shack sat behind and to his left. The cord on the path would do its work by morning. Trackers always follow what snags the eye.

By the time he climbed the cedar rise, the night had thinned. He sat with his back to a trunk and let memories pass in measured swells — heat, lash, chain, a mother's voice telling him to run. They shaped him; they did not direct his hands. Margaret's whisper about the rule slid in after them. He did not trust rules born from fires that were not his. He would not strike at whatever left those four gouges. He would use the fear of it, and let fear walk on two legs toward the wrong door.

An hour before gray-up, the river eased. A fox howled, twice. Jacob rose, brushed needles from his coat, and checked the lure. The cord lay damp with dew. Fresh, small prints crossed the path — light, angled, a hunter's tread. He smiled without showing teeth. Tala had seen what he left.

The shack door stuck a finger's width when he returned. Margaret slept at the table with her head on her arms, cloth still in hand. He slid the vial under the loose board and pressed it down with his heel. Light came thin through the birch.

There was time yet to pass by Collins's gate and let the herb tale find fresh ears; time to watch which way the preacher turned when the first voice cried, "Found something."

Jacob lifted the latch and took the narrow trail where riverweed snared a man's cuffs and cedar hooked a coat. Day would fill with questions. He had already placed the answers.

Behind him, birch shook a little wind and the shack's breathing faded. Out by the bend, water worked at stone. Deep in the cedar line, four long scores marked a trunk that was not his doing. He did not look at them again. He had work that bled and work that deceived, and both pointed away from claws.

Chapter 11

The scream came from the church steps and split the square in two.

By the time the Yorks reached the press of bodies, talk had hardened into accusation. Ropes hung from cart rails. A torch guttered in a brazier someone had dragged from the cooper's. Earnest took the edge of the throng with his bad leg set like a brace. "Eyes front," he told Cassandra, keeping her between himself and Iris. His hand dropped once to the knife at his belt and stayed there.

Iris scanned faces instead of shadows. "Where is Collins?" she said.

"By the door," someone muttered, and sure enough the reverend shouldered past two farmers, jaw taut, cloak unfastened as if he had come running.

Widow Hale burst from the narthex. “I saw it!” she cried, voice raw from a night without rest. “By the trees, reaching, speaking.” Her rosary broke in her hands and scattered into the muck.

Collins steadied her elbow. “Mary. Look at me.” His tone was calm, but his eyes kept sliding to the tree line west of the square.

“What did it say?” a man shouted.

“It was casting spells,” Mary whispered, pointing toward the pines. “There.”

The crowd swung as one. For a breath the square held still.

A figure stood just beyond the last fence post. Gaunt. Hooded. A tatter of cloak drifted where no branch moved. It lifted one shaking hand, and a dry croak pushed through split lips:

“Netsil ot evah uoy esaelp.”

The sound skittered over the square, thin at first, then stronger, the cadence strange but pleading:

“Hctiw a ton si reh-tom yim. Na-mow do-og a si esh. Reh nrub ton od.”

“Devil’s babble,” someone hissed.

A stone flew. It sailed through the figure as through smoke and smashed a shutter behind it.

Cassandra’s nails bit her palms. The tilt of the hood, the way the hand shook — something in those motions tugged at her with a familiarity she could not place. “It is the same one from the fence,” she whispered. Iris’s arm came across her shoulders without looking.

The figure lurched a step nearer. Dark tears, not water, tracked its cheeks. The voice raked the air again, hoarse and urgent:

"Yoov fo geb ee. Rel-lick eht see bo-caj. Hstayd all for el-bee-spon-ser see eh. Ah-lat ghin-dul-kin."

Murmurs snapped like twigs. "It names," a butcher growled. "It points and it names."

"Enough," Iris said, stepping so all could hear her. "If a thing speaks crooked, that is no proof of me." She lifted her chin and found Collins. "Reverend. You said we would look with our eyes."

A man shouldered past Earnest and swung a staff at Iris. Earnest caught the blow on his forearm, shoved the man off balance, and barked, "You will not lay hands on my wife." Two others crashed into him from the side. His knife skidded. A boot drove into his ribs. Air left him in a hard grunt.

"Stop," Collins shouted, forcing into the crush. "You will kill the wrong one."

The figure turned as if startled by his voice. The hood slipped. For an instant, when the light struck the ravaged face, several villagers flinched.

"It wears Iris's features," a woman breathed. "Her, only spent. A witch's shade."

Rope appeared. Hands seized Iris's wrists and dragged her toward the posts by the square well. "Hold," Collins called, but he was a man against a tide.

"Let her go," Cassandra cried. A woman caught her shawl. Iris twisted enough to slam an elbow backward; cartilage popped and a shriek split close by, but the pull toward the posts did not slacken.

The specter threw a last string of words at the howling square, voice breaking into a litany:

"Net-sil ton yoh leev yhw. Htayd er-om tnaw ton do ee. Gnih-try-veh tols eh-vah ee."

"Curse talk," a farmer spat, and raked a torch under the hemp. Pitch spoke its hot language. Flame licked up the fibers.

Collins reached the posts and seized the burning line. The jute chewed his palms. He ground the fire against wet earth and tore the knot low. "Back," he rasped to the torch man, who blinked through smoke and actually stepped away.

"Water," Iris coughed. "Cassie, bucket."

Cassandra lunged for the cooper's tub. The first throw sloshed more on the ground than on the rope, but steam jumped and the flame sulked. "Again," she shouted, and two bareheaded boys scrambled to either side of the tub with her.

Earnest, gray with pain, hooked an ankle and yanked a man flat. "Move," he snarled, dragging himself forward on his elbows.

For a fragile count of heartbeats the square faltered between shame and fury.

Then a voice at the back cried, "She fooled the rope. Burn the witch."

Another torch flared. Someone thrust Cassandra aside and kicked the bucket into the mud. A third man looped fresh twine, higher up, out of Collins's reach. The fire found it fast.

The specter stood at the fence line and did not move. It raised one hand as if to bless or warn. The hood tipped. In that tilt there was a likeness that made Cassandra's stomach ice over. The oldness of Iris's face, and yet not.

"Iris," Collins said, hoarse, "look at me."

She did not look at him. She looked at her daughter. "Stand, Cassie," she said, voice steady though smoke curled around her. "Stand and see this to its end."

Flame took her skirt. Heat leapt along the coarse fabric and climbed. The smell turned sharp and animal. The crowd pressed back from the licking edge, but no one cut the rope. Earnest threw himself at the post; three men dragged him off. Collins swung at the fresh twine with the iron handle of the brazier lid and missed. The next breath made his burned hands fail him.

"Rheh-seh-kat doolb," the specter croaked, its voice sinking into the roar like pebbles in a dark stream.

"Mother," Cassandra sobbed, flinging one last pan of water that flashed to steam before it touched the flame.

Iris's gaze never left her child. "Keep breathing," she said. "Keep walking."

The fire climbed to the ropes. Pitch snapped. A wash of heat bent the air. Iris arched once, drew a fierce breath that sounded like a pulled bellows, and went still.

The square fell quiet in the way places do when the worst part happens and there is nothing more to add. Torches guttered. Somewhere a child wailed. Someone dropped to their knees in the slop and started to pray without words.

At the edge of the square the figure lowered its hand. "Eh-reh ton si ek-it-sooj," it whispered, barely sound. Then it stepped backward into the line of pines and slid sideways into shadow. Branches did not stir where it passed.

Collins stood swaying, palms flayed, eyes wet from smoke. He looked at the faces around him and saw men and women trying to make a new story in their heads that hurt less than the one they had just made with their hands.

Earnest made a sound that did not belong to sea or land. He crawled to the post and laid his brow in the mud. Cassandra sank beside him and pressed both palms to the earth that had drunk the water she had brought too late.

Collins heard his own heartbeat in his ears and, beneath it, the echo of the croak:

"Net-sil ot eh-vah yoo eh-seh-elp. Ht-chee a ton see reh-thom eem. Reh n-ruhb ton od."

He turned toward the western trees. "May our Lord in heaven forgive us, for we know not what we do."

Earnest lifted his face. The skin at his mouth had gone hard as he rasped, "Why does God permit such tragedy?"

Collins's stomach jumped into his chest. He had heard of such things in the North; to see it in the flesh was hellish.

The crowd began to move again, slow and clumsy. Someone kicked sand over the brazier. Someone else righted the barrel that had been upended. No one let their eyes linger on the post.

Three figures stayed near the charred stake. Earnest lay half in the mud, tears cutting clean tracks through ash. Cassandra knelt beside him, sobbing, hands to her mouth. Collins stood behind them, head bowed, speaking a prayer too soft to carry.

At the shadowed fence line, the cause of it seemed still present: the same gaunt figure that had haunted the Yorks, its hooded face — just for an instant, in the angle of cheek and mouth — like Iris made older and ruined. Very faint, a last thread of sound drifted on the morning air, a plea turned inside out:

"Em eh-vahs. Net-sil. Eh-seh-elp."

Chapter 12

Sleep was a stranger clad in the inky tendrils of the barren pine branches that yawned beyond frostbitten windows. It crept in the shadows, a promise unfulfilled, taunting its captives with the ear-splitting shrieks of the dead that mingled with the memory of that fateful night in Danvers — a living nightmare, clawing at their skulls the same way the specter had reached for them from the forest. Voices swirled in Earnest's ears like the howling of wind against a restless sea, crashing into his mind with the same force of that wicked storm that had claimed his crewmates until he feared he may never know slumber again.

"Burn her!"

"Run, Cass!"

"Witch's kin!"

"Rheh-seh-kat doolb."

He jerked upright in bed, the barren space where Iris once rested beside him somehow colder now, more still in the pitch darkness, swallowing him with loneliness the same way that wretched curse had paralyzed him in the square as he helplessly watched his wife burn at the hands of the townsfolk. The blackened room sprawled before him, absent of the flowing cloaks, the dendritic fingers that stalked his sleepless mind like that specter on the fringe of the forest. It seemed to mock him with its emptiness, a disembodied cackle creeping through the cabin, teasing its presence yet offering no clemency in the form of manifestation.

"Leave me be!" he shouted at the abyss, only the icy whisper of wind leaking through cracked windows responding to his pleas. Tears burned in the creases of his sea-weathered face, scarring his flesh with his anguish like a slave branded by grief. There were no ghosts here, no spectral figures save for the skeletal pines whose shadows crawled across the ashen floor, backlit by a silver moon. That, and the phantom limb of his dead wife's sleeping figure beside him, forever a reminder of all he had lost, all he had tried to save. He lay back down, clutching the starchy sheets in a white-knuckled grasp as he repeated his demand to the darkness, defeated and weathered as a storm-worn ship. "Leave me be."

It was the same desperate refrain he had used when wrangling his daughter through the bloodthirsty crowd as Iris's burning flesh singed the air, clinging to his throat as he choked back his sobs and fought to protect the only kin he had remaining. He recognized that frenzied hatred well, those bloodshot eyes and spit-streaked shouts that pierced through his resolve as he shoved past the very townspeople who had once shown him mercy. They were the same suffocating stares, the same hateful cries that bled from the lips of those who had tried to take his wife in Danvers — only this time, they had succeeded.

He would not let them do so again with his daughter.

"Earnest, keep her." Iris's dying plea burned as fiercely as the flames that had claimed her as he took Cassandra's dainty hand into his own and dragged her through the muck and mire, back to the safety of their little cabin on the outskirts of Charleston. The crowd had satiated their hunger for retribution, had charred their witch to nothing more than a blackened mark in the muddy soil, but still their judgment loomed heavy as a thick fog over the heads of the two remaining Yorks. Escape was not an option; the prying eyes of the grief-stricken were still watching, still waiting to enact their justice on those they deemed responsible for stealing their children. If Earnest were to keep her as his burning wife had begged, it would have to be in the cabin, at least until he and Cassandra could run once more without the fear of being hunted.

Presently, Cassandra stirred from the tattered cot before the hearth, the once glowing embers now snuffed by the damp, wet rot that gnawed at the floorboards like a rabid dog feasting on bone. She clasped a woven blanket around her shoulders, shivering not only from the bitter cold that seeped through the cracks in the planks beneath her bare feet, but from the memory of that figure, its frayed cloaks billowing in the breeze, as familiar as they were frightening.

"Father?" Her tiny voice broke against the silence, a fractured whisper worn hoarse with unbridled tears that had scraped her throat raw. She haunted the foot of her father's bed, the ghost he had searched for in the shadows but did not find. A blind rage seized him at the sight of her, the sleep deprivation and sorrow stripping away his sensibilities until all that remained was the hollow imprint of that specter from the woods, its garbled tongue fuel to the fire that had turned his wife to ash.

"What do you want from me?" he screamed into the night, his weathered fingers pinched around Cassandra's shoulders like vices, undeterred by her tender yelps, her glassy eyes searching his through the pale moonlight, terrified and longing for comfort. All at once, the vision dissipated, a smoke lifted by the fear in his daughter's stare. He softened, fingers loosening from her small frame as the shame stitched itself into his bones, his gaze collapsing to the floor, unable to face the terror he had planted inside the one he was meant to keep. To protect. "I...I'm sorry, Cassie. Your mother...the flames...that thing in the woods. It haunts me so."

"It haunts me, too." Cassandra's words somehow carried more weight than the singed ropes that had lashed her mother's lifeless corpse to the stake, as though they were an incantation, though what spell she cast was still unclear, still unnamed. She hooked a trembling finger beneath her father's chin, forcing his eyes to find hers through the shadows that swam between them. "I feel it still. Calling. Reaching. I...I think it wants me. Same way it wanted Mother."

Her voice sparked icy fire in Earnest's gut, piercing him in the place he swore never to acknowledge. That same place where fear triumphed and men died at sea, where crowds surged like black tides and women burned under false names.

"Witch's kin!" Earnest shook the chorus from his mind, damned it back to the hellfire that threatened to take his family, his sanity.

"No," he growled, a promise rooted in the same will that had carried him south from Danvers. He blinked away the flames, the smoke, the specter's frayed shroud floating in the wind, willing his mind to free itself from the shackles that bound him to such torment. "It won't take you. I won't let it take you."

He wrapped his arms around his daughter, eyes stinging from the scent of soot that still clung to her skin from when Iris burned in the square, each ashy inhale a painful reminder of the townsfolk's ire. Cassandra's knees trembled beneath the weight of her father's grief, the embrace he had wanted to convey comfort and protection feeling more like a burden, a failure, though of what, she could not be certain. She only knew that she could feel its pull, its fingers reaching out from the dense forest, marking her.

"Rheh-seh-kat doolb."

"Stand, Cassie." Her mother's final words coiled in her ear like smoke clawing free from the pyre where she smoldered to nothing more than an inky mound of singed flesh and blackened bone. She wanted to be strong, to stand tall, but she found no purchase in the floorboards that bit her feet, only splintered edges stabbing her skin like the townspeople had pierced her with accusation in their eyes, holding her down as she fought to reach her mother.

"I'm scared, Father," she whimpered into Earnest's chest, the admission even more chilling in the darkened room than the relentless wind that shrieked through the cracks in the windows. "Danvers, Charleston — it matters not where we go. We are marked for death. It follows us still. I feel it."

Earnest stiffened at the words, the protestations dying in his throat with the memory of the hollow stares from the Charleston crowd, their hungry hands reaching through time as though delivered from Danvers. In the caverns of his heart, her words rang true, try as he might to silence them, to reverse their meaning. Mossy teeth and crooked mouths flashed inside his mind, each of them spewing filth from forked tongues that frothed with unabashed fury.

"Burn her!"

"Witch's kin!"

"Rheh-seh-kat doolb."

But there was another voice, too—a faint flicker in the shadows, a soft glimmer in the darkness that held something like hope, though he dared not name it so. Still, it called to him as a bright mark staining the horizon at the edge of a raging sea, promising the shore.

"Stop! Lord's mercy, stop!" Reverend Collins's voice had cut through the square like a blade slashing through flesh.

"She's no witch! Reason, damn you!" The words hadn't been mere placation; there had been real conviction in his pleas as he ripped the torch from the villager's grasp, as though the priest somehow knew what the rest of his parish did not. It was the kind of knowing that only lived in the minds of those who had seen the truth but were too afraid to speak it. Earnest had recognized that same certainty etched into the reverend's stare when he had come to the cabin just days before, the weight of it betraying his duplicity. But the sailor was no fool.

He would tear the truth from the priest's throat, even if he had to carve it out with his whalebone knife, its blade stained red with the gospel of the true villain — the keeper of children lost to the night.

"Marked not," Earnest croaked, vengeance a tight knot caught in his throat, scraping at his tongue until his words tasted of copper and iron. "The reverend knows. Heard him in the crowd."

Cassandra peeled away from her father's grasp, thin trails of grief shining softly in the moonlight as they streaked through the remnants of mud and ash on her pale face. "But the others," she said, shivering at the memory of those greedy hands that grabbed at her in the square. "They care not what he knows. They only—"

"Hush, child," Earnest snapped, his voice a whip, cracking through the shadows, lashing the backs of anyone who dared doubt his reason. He stood from the bed, limping through the darkness, ignoring the anguished cries from his leg as he hobbled to the table where his blade glinted in the moonlight, its worn handle beckoning to him, soothing his heartache with the promise of retribution. Pocketing the weapon, he turned to his daughter, fire blazing in his eyes, not from the flames that took his wife but from the embers stoked afresh in his gut, roiling with the truth yet unspoken, the admission he would tear free by whatever means necessary.

"No more running." He jutted a crooked finger toward the window, his shadow stretching across the hardwood, wraith-like, as if he, too, were a specter reaching through the woods. "We stand now. The reverend will hear our pleas. He'll end this curse, one way or another."

Cassandra said nothing, only bowed her head and obliged her father's wishes to don her coat and stuff her tender feet inside her mud-caked boots. As they pressed into the night, icy wind nipping at exposed skin, pines clawing overhead like skeletal hands reaching from unmarked graves, she kept her eyes on the forest's edge, that gaunt figure creeping somewhere in the trees, unseen but watching.

Always watching.

Chapter 13

The forest swallowed light, its pines thrusting blackened limbs into a sky choked with ash, the bitter scent of burned flesh still lingering in the night's harsh chill. It clung to the back of the Yorks' throats as they stumbled over gnarled roots and mud-caked earth to find the reverend's house through the darkness. Clapboard houses stood like tombstones against an inky sky, the only sign of life within the whispers of smoke that curled up from the chimneys to the silver moon overhead. Boots squelched against damp soil that gripped at Cassandra's feet like the hands that had grabbed at her in the square as she watched her mother burn. She trailed her father's uneven gait, his wounded leg forcing a slow, painful pace past the churchyard where the townsfolk had pinned her to the ground, her mother's final command nothing more than a fractured refrain echoing from somewhere deep inside.

"Stand, Cass!" She shivered at the memory, the eerie quiet of the sleeping town somehow even more unsettling in the aftermath of what had happened there, deceptive in its silence — a wolf stalking the pastures, slinking through the tall grass, waiting to sink its teeth into hide. As they neared the steeple, sharp breath hitched in her throat, her eyes falling on the charred rubble, the singed ropes lying in loose coils like dead snakes piled atop her mother's remains. Earnest clapped a rugged hand against her lips, his callused fingers pressing firm against chapped skin worn raw from the cold.

"It ain't her," he muttered low, the words a repeat from his earlier shouts into a frenzied crowd, this time softened by grief yet weighted with warning. "Stay close. We're nearly there."

Cassandra nodded against her father's hand, swallowing down the whimper that threatened to burst forth like a sparking ember crackling from a burning hearth. The night pressed in, thick and heavy as her father held her mouth tight, the dead air pressing in, cautioning her against letting grief spill forth. She clutched Earnest's coat with freezing fingers, refusing to look back at the pile of ash and bone and smoldered skin, not daring to glance at the forest's edge where the specter had rasped in its mangled tongue.

"Rheh-seh-kat doolb."

The Yorks pressed on in choked silence, their sleepless minds a tangled knot of anguish and despair, nothing but the river's quiet babble through the darkened wood to guide them through the night. *Closer, closer*, it beckoned them forth, past the church, past the cemetery, down to the edge of the town, where the Collins' house reached out from cracked earth like a rotted hand clawing forth from an unmarked grave. A bitter breeze carried the scent of damp rot that wafted from the home's splintered timber, the fog of earthen decay joining the stench of dank soil that hung in the mud-slick yard. Cracked pavers offered small purchase as Cassandra and Earnest negotiated their way through the slippery earth, their boots smeared with filth, soggy with frost and muck. Through the warped shutters, a sliver of candlelight bled into the shadows, hinting at the worried mind that lay awake within, as restless as the visitors that came unbidden to its doorstep.

"Stay back," Earnest growled, stilling Cassandra at the edge of the porch, his weight a symphony of creaking planks that cried in protest beneath his footsteps as he crossed to the door. Knuckles cracked against wood, announcing the Yorks' arrival like thunder in the night, the pounding fist an echo of Cassandra's thrumming heart. Her ears rang in the absence of sound as her father's hand fell to his side, his fingers brushing the whalebone handle of his blade — eager, thirsty for answers, for vengeance. She watched as the door screeched open, the flood of amber light from the fire burning within the cabin casting harsh shadows across the threshold, the old priest nothing more than a wilted silhouette, his hands trembling slightly as he raised a lantern high to better appraise his uninvited guests.

"Earnest? Wh–what are you doing here at such an hour?" His voice pitched high, tenor warbling as unsteadily as the light that shone from his torch that swayed from shaking fingers. "Y–you shouldn't be here. You shouldn't—"

"Enough!" Earnest shouted, jaw rigid, eyes like lightning, humming with electric intensity as he closed the distance between himself and the reverend. His fingers curled around the knife handle the same way a drowning sailor might reach for a life raft — desperate, hungry. "My wife is dead, Collins. Murdered because of *your* town. *Your* parish. But you know the truth. Seen it in your eyes when you come to our cabin. Heard it in the square when you tried to talk reason. And I ain't leavin' this porch 'till I hear you say it."

Silence stretched like a black cloud, swollen with rain, drenched in unspoken truth that stayed trapped inside the reverend's throat, the veins in his neck bulging, twitching, straining beneath the weight of Earnest's stare. His mind drifted again to Margaret, her pallor replaced by an inexplicable glow, too rosy, too near to Ellie's scream, to Ruth's loss, to Thomas's disappearance. That strange vigor twisted in his gut, a hangman's knot tightening around his doubt, forcing him to face the widower's gaze, his black eyes beseeching him to speak aloud that which he did not dare to think.

"I...I do not know what you mean." The lie tasted like rust on his tongue, images of that red-stained bead along the riverbank flashing in his mind as the copper tang mingled in his mouth with the guilt. Earnest lunged, hands like vices around the priest's collar, eyes like daggers, piercing through thinly masked deception as easily as a scythe through fields of wilted cotton. The sailor's breath stung hot and wrathful on Collins's cheeks, full of the same fire that had engulfed the healer in the churchyard, her dying pleas snuffed out beneath the roar of flames.

"Save your lies for your sermons." Earnest's voice scratched against the reverend's ear, sharp and jagged as the cracked fingernails that dug into the paper skin above his collarbone. "That forked tongue might work on your flock, but it won't fool me. I see your mind at work; the truth gnaws at you. Speak it now, or I'll carve it from you. Feed you to the river to drown with the beast you protect."

A spark of silver flashed in the widower's eyes, as sharp and menacing as the knife that caught the candlelight and reflected the priest's fate in his stare. Collins shook, lips moist with sweat and tears that flowed in salty pools down his chin, dripping down to the callused hands that stilled him against the doorframe. From behind him, he could hear the gentle rise and fall of his wife's breath as she slept in the other room, each rush of air stained with the distant sound of a mother's grief, a child's laughter lost to the wind, a fire's roar deafening the dying pleas of a woman falsely accused. And beneath it all was that shack that stood slumped and broken by the river's bend, glowing red as the embers that fueled the anger burning bright within Earnest's deadly stare.

He could not cast the shroud of suspicion on Margaret, could not bear to see her blackened flesh join that of the healer's in the churchyard, no matter how much her unnatural flush pulled at his mind, a loose thread unraveling him from within. But Jacob...Jacob was a different story, a necessary sacrifice, if only to pacify the seething sailor at his doorstep.

"Speak! Now!" Earnest repeated his demand, Cassandra's soft yelp a muted cry beneath clamped hands as she watched from the muddy yard below. Collins swallowed hard, teeth chattering not from the chill that snaked down his neck and seeped into his skin beneath his gauzy cotton sleepshirt, but from the icy terror that tugged at his conscience, the waves of Margaret's breath crashing like an arctic ocean against his body. All at once, his jaw unhinged, tongue loosened around a half-truth, the only offering he could make that might still preserve his happiness, his sanity.

"Jacob." The choked whisper fell like a curse in the night, its strangled rasp a rope pulled taut, snapping with the weight of a man now marked for death. Earnest's fingers slackened around the reverend's collar, a spell not broken but recast to that russet scar on the river's bend, that reddish glow too close to his cabin. He hobbled backward, ignoring the searing pain that shot through his leg and threatened to buckle his knees.

"We go together." It was not a request, but a demand written in the blood that pulsed like liquid fire within his veins, driving him to the brink of madness, where reason gave way to recrimination.

"I...yes. Yes, of course," Collins spluttered, thinking better than to deny the sailor's requisition lest he reach for that whalebone hilt and sink its blade into his quivering flesh. "I will call for you in the morning, and we will—"

"No!" Earnest barked, the sound reverberating through the priest's chest where his heartbeat once rattled in his ribcage like a bird fresh for the reaping. "I'll not wait a second longer to avenge my Iris. This ends now."

The reverend's protest died on his tongue as he retreated back into his cabin, his figure pinned beneath the watchful eye of the widower looming at his open door. He stuffed his bare feet hastily inside a pair of wrinkled boots, threaded bony arms through the coat that hung beside the mantle, the fabric somehow damp and cold despite the warmth that radiated from the hearth. With a lantern dangling from his frail fingers, he slipped into the darkness to join the Yorks beyond. As he shut the door behind him, his mind snagged on Margaret's breath, that gentle hum of sleep arresting his heart, reminding him of the secrets he still kept, the life he chose to protect, and the souls he failed to save because of them.

"Lord, forgive me," he muttered to the moon, the stars still buried somewhere beneath the sprawling pines, the smoky fog that filled the sky, tasting of ash and death. No answer came to him; just the scuffling of boots through brittle leaves and mud-soaked earth, and that quiet babble from the river, its coarse whisper eating the silence with its promise.

Closer, closer.

Chapter 14

The path twisted through the forest, mired and scarred, roots jutting like bones through muddy earth. Their bark peeled wet in the gloom where shadows pooled too thick, engulfing the silver strands of moonlight that wove through the looming pines overhead, their branches casting claw-like silhouettes upon the trio as they navigated through the wilds. The reverend led the group, guided by the river's pulse, its steady whisper — *closer, closer* — quickening his pace, thrumming in his ears, gnawing at his mind as Margaret's flush hinted at truths he'd die before speaking. Truths that lingered in the shack's red glow as he came upon it at the riverbend, the Yorks trailing closely behind.

"There." His breath was a mist haunting the darkened wood, shrouding his knobby finger like a specter in the night as he pointed to the dilapidated dwelling, its scarlet shadow like a bloodstain on the riverbank. Earnest forged ahead, boots grinding through leaves and mud, each step a wet crunch echoing off the pines. His bloodied leg throbbed dully beneath the wool, a limp he forced steady with grit alone. The axe wound seeped fresh through the fabric, staining it dark where mud clung wet and cold. His coat hung torn, mud-streaked, blood-crusted from the square's chaos. The whalebone knife gleamed in his fist, its edge sharp with a vengeance carved by Iris's ashes, her final plea a fire searing his skull, driving him through the wilds' dark heart to the shack's festering rim.

Cassandra followed close, shawl frayed at the edges, eyes raw and hollow from sleeplessness. Deep crescents carved into her palms where jagged nails dug through paper skin, grief and fear a weight dragging her steps, forming strange images in the inky tendrils that snaked through the trees, hinting at the secrets buried deep within its clutches.

"Rheh-seh-kat doolb." The specter's cry was a noose tightening her throat, its echo clawing her marrow since the homestead's fence, sharper now as the dark pressed in. She fixed her gaze on the reverend's flickering lantern, her father's unsteady gait as they tracked closer to the shack, the scent of death wrapping itself around them like thick ropes, lashing them to a fate that remained unseen.

The tiny cabin crouched ahead, a festering wound gouged into the forest's flesh. Its walls were warped with planks patched with rot, sagging beneath a roof of moss and broken thatch that glistened in the dreary darkness. Gaps yawned dark where the wind hissed through, carrying a reek of blood and damp earth, sharp enough to sting the nose and gag the throats of the visitors that crept unwanted to the doorstep. Wood moaned beneath mud-caked boots as they climbed the porch, the butcher's stench from within a wicked greeting, the stink snapping taut the loose threads in Cassandra's mind as she recalled that first encounter along the river she'd fled weeks back. A faint glow pulsed within, meek candlelight flickering through cracks, casting jagged slashes across the floorboards like blood frozen mid-fall, snagging Earnest's memory of the red glow he'd tracked nights past, a wound throbbing west he'd sworn to carve open.

He slowed, jaw tight beneath a bead streaked with soil and sweat. His grip tightened on the knife as he scanned the dark, pines rustling around them, their branches like gnarled hands reaching for the moon. Shadows writhed in faint rivulets beneath as if breathing, a menace he felt in his marrow since the square's smoke choked the dawn.

"That smell," he growled, voice rough, sea-worn, cracking against the wind's low howl. His eyes narrowed, tracing the shack's silhouette against the pines, dread coiling cold as Iris's ashes flashed sharp in his skull. Beside him, Collins's blood frosted over in his limbs, the reek of death that wafted from within too palpable to ignore, the taste of it undeniable. His breath swirled in a fevered haze around the tang of it, Margaret's unnatural glow seizing his senses as he steadied his stance and prepared to face what he knew all along but could not stomach.

Cassandra's breath hitched, her voice cracked low. "Blood, like before." Her gaze darted. Shadows shifted beyond the trees, too tall, too still. She tensed, frayed cloaks and mangled voices snagging at her mind, dragging her back to the foot of the pyre where her mother burned, that specter's curse fueling the frenzy and the flames.

A twig snapped to their left. Not wind. Clean, close, deliberate. Earnest stilled with the door half-shouldered. Cassandra's head turned toward the sound and caught a flash in the brambles — a thin binding of feather and sinew snagged on thorn, the kind Tala wore at her wrist.

"Run, Cass!" Iris's scream from Danvers was a shard piercing her skull now as she stood huddled between her father and the priest, resolve flickering beneath her grief, boots rooted to the planks beneath her feet, frozen with fear. Earnest nodded, silent, his jaw clenching tighter. His hand shot out, steadying her with a grip rough but sure. Protest died on the reverend's tongue as he watched the sailor push the door, its hinges groaning, a low wail splitting the quiet as it swung wide.

"Go," Earnest hissed, pushing into the shack.

The stench within flooded thick with iron and rot, a butcher's mark that strangled their senses, left them breathless, forced them to seek refuge in raised coat collars, the bite of fear-soaked sweat preferable to that of the coppery tang that greeted them from the shack. Blood pooled fresh on the floorboards within, glistening black in the candle's frail glow. The flame wavered in sporadic bursts as if trembling from the sight of what it illuminated. A shadow stretched too long across the walls, its wiry arms like the looming pines that cradled the cabin in their claws. Collins clamped a shaky hand over his unhinged mouth, the sight of Jacob standing at the heart of the shadow, cloak sodden with mud and blood, grin glinting red where crimson streaked his chin, too much for the priest to bear.

"Too late," Jacob snarled, voice thick with relish, rasping low like distant thunder. His hands gripped a knife, its blade dulled with gore. A strip of flesh dangled from his fist, raw and dripping as he chewed slow, savoring the wet snap between his teeth. Blood dribbled down his jaw to spatter the floorboards, the hunger in his stare mirroring the pull in Earnest's gut that he'd felt since the churchyard whispers. He felt it sharper now as Jacob's eyes gleamed, wild and edged with a predator's delight, stepping forward as the candle flared.

"You took her!" Earnest's roar tore raw, grief and fury a tide crashing through his chest as he lunged, whalebone hilt in hand, blade arcing for Jacob's throat with a force that burned his arm. Collins darted back, his calls to reason a futile plea, deafened by the clashing of steel against steel.

Jacob twisted fast, his knife meeting Earnest's with a spark that flared bright in the gloom. The force shuddered up Earnest's arm as Jacob laughed, low and cruel.

"Framed you good. Burned your witch!" His boot slammed Earnest's wounded leg, pain shooting hot through the wool, buckling him to one knee with a grunt that rasped raw in his throat. Mud and blood smeared the boards beneath him. His grip trembled on the knife as Jacob's grin widened, a taunt tethered to the whalebone twin he'd planted in the square, a noose Earnest felt tightening since the mob's roar swallowed Iris's stand.

Cassandra screamed, "Father!"

She lurched forward through the shadows, scrabbling for a broken plank leaning against the wall. Its splintered edge bit her palms, where blood welled in shallow pools as she swung it with a force that cracked Jacob's shoulder. Wood snapped loudly against bone. The butcher grunted, backhanding his assailant with a slap that rang sharp. Cassandra crumpled against the wall, boards groaning as she fell, her eyes raw with grief and rage as she clawed the floor. Jacob's shadow swallowed her crouched figure, his demented grin deepening as he raised his knife, ready to feed his blade afresh. Before he could claim another innocent's soul, add to the blood pooled at his feet and in his mouth, a shadow burst through, cloak swaying, beads glinting dully in the candle's flicker.

It was Tala.

"Enough. Your blood ends this!" Her eyes blazed, fierce and dark with a hunter's resolve as she drew her bow taut, arrow notched, aiming at Jacob. She loosed her arrow, the sharp edge hissing through the air, grazing his arm with a wet slice. Blood spurted from the wound as he ducked, grinning wider. His cloak snapped as he shifted, a wild beast dodging prey he'd sworn to outlast. He laughed low like a blade on stone, the sound tied to the Wendigo legends she'd tracked since Kael's beads scattered the window's shack.

Earnest roared, lunging up from his knee. His knife slashed wildly, missing Jacob's throat. Steel sliced the air, then flesh — Tala's chest. Her arrow clattered to the floor, blood blooming fast, dark and wet through her hides as she staggered, eyes widening in shock.

"No, not me." Her voice broke, a gasp fading as she fell. Beads scattered across the floorboards, glinting in the candlelight like stars fallen too soon. Her bow snapped under her weight with a dull crack that split the quiet. She gurgled softly as blood pooled beneath her, staining the wood dark.

"What have you done?" Collins croaked from the shadows, moonlight spilling in fearful ribbons through his eyes as he thought of the tribesmen, their battle cry a well-worn echo etched into the trees — *blood for blood* — prophesying the sailor's doom. Earnest froze, knife trembling in his grip, horror stabbing his gut.

"God, no," he choked, blood dripping from the blade to spatter the floor. His hands shook as he sank beside the huntress. Tala's eyes fluttered, her resolve breaking under the weight of his missed strike, a tragedy he'd carved with his own hand.

"Earnest, keep her." Iris's dying wish shattered in the shack's rot, Earnest's chest heaving as grief sank its claws deeper. Jacob bolted, cloak snapping sharp as he shoved past Collins, the door banging wide as he laughed, his cackle peeling through the wind.

"Yours now!"

His boots thudded fast through the mud, splashing wet as he melted into the pines, shadows swallowing him whole. The wind's howl cloaked his escape like a shroud too thick to pierce, his grin a taunt lingering in the moonlit canopy, lips and teeth a wreath of herbs planted purposefully in the square, igniting the flames that claimed Earnest's wife.

"He's gone. Lord, forgive me." Collins broke into a sob, the consequences of his half-truth soaking scarlet into the woodgrain, unraveling him from within, a weight he'd carried since Margaret's eyes sparkled unnaturally in the pews after the first child was claimed by the butcher's wrath.

Cassandra crawled, breath ragged in the dark. "Father, she's..." Her voice cracked, hands shaking as she reached for Tala. Blood slicked her palms where it pooled warm and fading, grief a tide drowning her anew as she clutched the hunter's arm. Her beads flashed in the candlelight, a loss tied to Iris's pyre forever bound to one another, her sob rasping raw and hollow in the night.

Footfalls crunched sharply from beyond the open door, too late to stem the bleeding, to stitch the loss. Four souls stood apart, their shadows long and fractured, their hearts pounding a rhythm older than the pines. Tala's body lay cold on the shack floor, her throat gashed, beads scattered along the planks, obscured by the silhouettes of her tribe, her father's stoic gaze crumbling at the sight of his daughter's mangled form. A wail rose from the women who flanked his sides, the noise raw and shattering, drenched in grief, knees buckling to kiss the earth, hands turning crimson in the glistening pool that soaked the floor as Anah and Mira clambered to Tala's side.

"Hassun, it's not—" Collins's plea fell on deaf ears, dread sinking cold as the tribe leader's empty gaze consumed him. The Native's staff pounded against the floor, the dull tip sodden with mud and the blood of a daughter he could not save.

Hassun filled the doorway like a tree that had always been there and only now stepped forward. Snow-gray braids hung to his chest. The carved staff in his hand touched the threshold once, a hollow sound that pulled every breath in the room tight.

He went first to his daughter. Fingers brushed hair from Tala's cheek, then found the last warmth at her throat. When he lifted his hand, it glistened dark. He did not look at the others yet. He set that palm upon the boards, pressed it into the tacky print where a blade had kissed wood, then laid it gently over the wound blooming in her chest, as if to close it with touch alone.

The women behind him began to keen, a low river of grief that rose and fell against the shack's thin walls. Collins tried a word and failed, the sound breaking in his mouth. Earnest lifted both empty hands, then pointed toward the door Jacob had torn open, then to himself, then shook his head. The motion died in the air between them.

Hassun's gaze traveled at last. Knife on the floor. Blood stringing the grain. Cassandra's skirt smudged where she had crawled. The hunter's beads scattered like dull stars around the body. He read the room as a tracker reads snow. His staff thumped a measured beat, once, twice, again, as if marking time for a rite only he knew.

He spoke, not to them but to the dead and to the pines listening outside. The words were round with breath and winter. He drew a sign before his ribs with two fingers, the old mark of a hunger that eats what it loves and cannot stop. The staff came down a final time.

"Wendigo."

Two archers lifted their bows a hand's breadth. Another hunter dragged a thumb slow along his own throat and let the threat hang in the smoke. Collins stepped forward, palms open, pleading in a language that went nowhere. Earnest, still kneeling, reached as if the gesture itself could bridge the space, then let his arm fall. Cassandra pressed knuckles to her lips and made no sound at all.

Hassun did not advance. He went to one knee beside Tala and gathered her to him the way a father gathers a child who has fallen asleep by the fire. He spoke again, softer, and the women answered. Together they worked a woven cloth from a pack, laid it under her, lifted by corners, lifted by love. Beads clicked faintly against the plank where they slipped free and rolled to rest.

At the threshold he paused. The staff raised and pointed once at Earnest. Not a question. A naming. Then the tribe receded into the trees as they had come, grief moving with them like weather, leaving the shack small and cold in their wake, the candle trembling in its tin cup, the air emptied of everything but iron and the echo of a word that would not lose its hold.

Chapter 15

Night clawed the wilds beyond Charleston, a black shroud pierced only by the jagged dance of torchlight as Hassun led the Yorks back to his camp, Collins and the tribeswomen following close behind. Flames hissed and spat in a wind thick with pine resin and the rot that billowed from the open shack by the riverbend, the scent of Tala's blood still fresh in the air, a solemn reminder of her unwilling sacrifice and the Wendigo that haunted the woods. Pines loomed like sentinels, skeletal, their branches twisted into claws that raked a moonlit sky, swaying as if alive with a hunger older than the earth beneath. Spanish moss draped low, gray tendrils beaded with frost, each drip striking the mud like blood frozen mid-fall in the fire's frail light.

They came upon a hollow, a circle of stones ringing the clearing, smooth and ancient, their faces stained dark by old rites. The air pressed down, bitter haze curling from a pit at the center where embers pulsed under charred herbs — sage and yarrow. Their tang soured on Earnest's tongue, an echo of the spark that had lit the square and taken Iris. His hand went to the absence at his belt, to the whalebone that lay now in Tala's chest. The true butcher laughed somewhere in the pines, lost to the wind.

Natives ringed the stones, cloaks shifting in the breeze, beadwork winking in the half-light, eyes rimmed in grief and rage. Staffs beat earth in a low thunder, a rhythm that sank into the bones. The chant rose, old words braided with mourning.

Hassun stood at the head, tall and unbowed, raven feathers whispering against his shoulders. He lifted his staff and brought it down once. Silence fell like a blade. His gaze fixed on Earnest, who knelt bound within the stones, twine biting his wrists the way fire had bitten Iris. Tala's broken bow lay near Hassun's feet, sinew sprung and curled like a severed vein.

Earnest's coat hung torn, mud and blood crusting its wool. The axe wound throbbed, seeping fresh. He met the chief's stare and then looked past him to his daughter. Iris's last words burned clear.

"Earnest, keep her."

He swallowed smoke. "I didn't mean to kill her," he said, sea-worn voice rough against the chant's rise. "Jacob's the butcher."

Torches spit and hissed. The pines listened. He had weathered storms and ropes and the drag of tides, but this land's hunger was slower, deliberate, grinding hope to grit.

"Let me prove it!" he cried, but the rhythm only swelled.

Cassandra stood at the rim, gripped by two warriors. Her shawl hung in tatters. Sleep had not touched her eyes. Blood dried under her nails from the shack's floor; Tala's fall replayed — arrow clatter, startled gasp, her father's blade catching wrong. The chant pressed close. Her mother's voice threaded through it.

Strength's in you, Cassie. Stand always.

She watched Hassun set his feet, weight forward, staff angled to strike. She saw the rope at her father's wrists, the way his bad leg trembled. She understood, all at once, how the next heartbeat would end.

"No," she said, and her voice broke the chant for a single, human moment.

She did not ask. She did not bargain.

She tore free, skin burning under the hands that tried to hold her. Mud slipped underfoot. She hit the ring at a run, shoulder driving into Earnest's chest hard enough to knock breath and prayer from him. He toppled, ropes and all, out of the stones. She dropped in his place before anyone could reach her.

The staff fell.

Sound cracked the clearing. Light surged up through the seams in the earth and through the gaps between the stones, white as lightning, hot as a kiln. Cassandra's head snapped back; her cry was glass shattering in a gale. Wind ripped through the circle, snapping cloaks and beating torches sideways, the blast snapping the cords at Earnest's wrists where he sprawled in the mud. He reached for her. His fingers closed on smoke.

Then stillness.

Only the soft drift of ash. Only the shawl, collapsed in a tattered heap where she had knelt.

"Cassie!" Earnest's roar tore the hush. He crawled, hands gouging wet ruts, eyes wild, face streaked with soot and salt. The ring had already gone dull, stones slick with dew and something darker.

Around him the tribe stilled. Some backed away, cloaks lifting in the eddying wind. Others sank to their knees and bowed their heads. Hassun's staff tapped once against stone; his shoulders sagged.

The elder stared at the shawl, fingers clenched around her bowl until it shook. "She is gone," she said, voice blown thin. "Where we cannot follow."

The torches guttered. Pines moaned overhead. Earnest gathered the shawl as if it still held weight, as if warmth might return to it by will alone. His voice broke on the old prayer and never found its ending.

"Not her. God, not her."

Smoke lifted in slow ribbons. Stones gleamed wet. Blood and ash sealed Cassandra's absence like a lid. From the treeline a whisper threaded the dark, low at first, then needling higher through needles and boughs, a chant reborn and wrong.

"Rheh-seh-kat doolb."

The tribe melted to shadow one by one, grief carried quiet between them. Earnest knelt alone in the churned mud, breath juddering, hands black with earth, the echo of the curse tightening around him like a rope that would never slacken.

Chapter 16

Darkness swallowed Cassandra, a void thick as tar, crushing her chest until her ribs groaned, each breath like a jagged tooth catching in her throat, a fish hooked too deep to free. The ritual's curse had torn her from the clearing, its light flaring, blinding, searing her eyes until tears streaked in warm rivers down her cheeks, bitter with salt and iron as the anguish collected on her tongue. She choked on a scream, the noise fraying into a silence that pressed heavier than the shadows, swallowing sound and sense.

Her blood-soaked shawl snapped in the wind, its damp weight anchoring her down, the threads unraveling with her thoughts. The ropes that had been used to bind Earnest in the circle now bit into her wrists, grinding into her flesh until blood welled beneath her cloak's worn cuffs, warm and slick, a reminder of the clearing's chaos, of Earnest's roar, of the elder's hands smearing symbols on her cheeks as the air itself turned traitor. A cold, thick fog loomed heavy with smoke and rotting leaves, curling in her lungs like a suffocating tide. She stood within a circle, ash and blood smeared in spirals along the forest floor, pulsing like the symbols burned into her skin, their heat a living thing beneath her flesh, clawing at her bones.

Beyond the circle, the world twisted, seemingly unmaking itself. The pines overhead released their grip on a dusky horizon, their branches bending upward, needles rising to boughs as if time wept backward, the sky flickering from dusk to dawn, then night, healing itself until the light returned. Voices slurred into garbled chants, the words grating on Cassandra's ears, sharp as broken glass. The river pulsed from somewhere in the brightened woods, a hum snaking through her marrow, tugging at her bones with a hunger she'd felt since fleeing the riverbank...how long ago had it been now? Days? Years? Suddenly, she couldn't remember, as if time itself had become undone.

Her heart thudded, a drumbeat thrashing against the silence as she clung to the circle's ash, its faint glow a tether in the void in which she found herself. What was this place? Iris's face flashed before her eyes, her steely gaze a stark contrast to the softness in her voice as she spoke by the wagon's wheel.

"Steady, Cassie." Guilt sank cold in her gut, a stone dropped into the glassy surface of a frozen river. Had she failed her mother already?

She flailed, nails splitting against nothing, blood streaking her fingers to spatter the earth at her feet. Her boots sank into mud, but beyond the circle's rim, the ground shifted, unraveling before her eyes as though a force beyond her comprehension somehow breathed life back into the wilds. Panic gnawed at her chest as she scurried to the circle's edge, her fingers trembling slightly as she extended them past the border. Pain seared her hand, the skin outside the circle turning wrinkled, veins bulging, nails yellowing and cracking instantaneously before her eyes. She gasped, yanking her hand back, and the aging ceased, her skin restored, smooth and young, as if untouched. Her heart pounded, terror a tide dragging her out to an untamed sea. What was this curse? She tested it again, stepping out, placing one foot beyond the ash, then the other. A shudder tore through her body, her hair graying, strands snapping in the wind, joints creaking as the years piled on. She bent down to the earth, her hands raking the damp soil, eyes sinking to a puddle, the smooth surface betraying her youth with a warped reflection. Sunken eyes and hollowed cheeks stared back, a hag's face that appeared both frightening and familiar — a specter lingering in her skull.

"Blood calls blood." The elder's voice echoed from within the circle, but outside, the words were disjointed, a reversed hymn that scratched at Cassandra's mind as a terrible realization took hold. Though the ritual had been meant for her father, she had been bound instead, cursed to a world unmaking itself around her, the backward passage of time somehow devouring her, aging her in moments. Within the confines of the ancient stones, she stood preserved, unaged, her thoughts pressing forward as she watched the world beyond the circle slip further back in time, the pines unswaying, voices unspoken, moments unraveling. At night, her shadow lingered, a specter others glimpsed, born of the ground's strange air, heavy with the ritual's weight. When she dared to step out, she paid the price, her body a warning, an omen older than the trees.

What has become of me? The thought tugged at her mind, tortured her with its persistence. Through the dread, memories of her mother surfaced — her laughter by the creek, fingers threading through tangled hair as she fashioned braids from unruly tresses. Hope sparked, an undying ember burning softly within the confines of her heart. If she could step beyond the circle, go back to the moment before the pyre in the square, could she prevent the flames from burning? Could she learn the circle's rules, break this curse before the wilds claimed her? Claimed them both?

Time snapped.

The square blazed, flames receding from unburned wood, the hiss of embers dissolving into silence. Smoke unwound, curling back into the stake where Iris stood, her body rising, uncharred, her skirt whole, untouched by the fire that had reduced her to nothing more than a blackened pile of ash and bone. Her hair smoothed, soot fading, strands returning to gold, glinting in a dawn unbroken by the crowd's fury.

"Eissac, dnats." A garbled cry spilled from her mother's lips, slurred and reversed, her eyes brightening as she stepped backwards from the stake, ropes unfastening themselves, her frame straightening into steel. The crowd slipped back, shrieks fading, torches dimming, the black smoke no longer stinging Cassandra's lungs. Earnest's knees unbuckled from the earth, blood retreating to his nose as though healing itself.

"Ti t'nia ehs!" His roar was a chant, twisting through the square, that same reverse speech that mangled her mother's words. And there beside the cart, small frame pressed into the muck, Cassandra saw herself, younger, the scream returning to her throat, shawl mending, hands unclenching, eyes draining of the terror that had stretched them wide. Again, her mother's voice called above the crowd.

"Reh peek, tsenrae." The slurred words stretched across space and time, Cassandra watching it unfold from within the circle, boots sinking into mud that lifted beyond the rim's reach, cloak heavy with mire. Her heart ached as hope surged anew; Iris was alive, unburned, her defiance unbroken by the crowd's ire. Could she warn them, keep their hungry hands from lashing her mother to the post, branding her a witch, ripping her life away?

Guilt sank its claws deeper as memories tugged at Cassandra's mind — her mother's hand, callused but gentle, teaching her knots by the wagon's wheel, her laughter a warmth lost to the pyre's blaze. The elder's symbols pulsed on her skin, a reminder of the ritual's price. She could not stand idle. If there was a chance to unseal her mother's fate, she would have to leave the circle. She steeled herself, breath held in a vice within her chest as she stepped beyond the rim, pain searing as time ravaged her, skin sagging, hair whitening, voice rasping raw, frame buckling under decades piled in moments.

"Stop! She's innocent!" she screamed, hand raised, but the sound died in her throat, her vocal cords twisting out a mangled curse instead, those same words that had haunted her since the square's chaos.

"Rheh-seh-kat doolb." The chant she did not will churned raw and ancient from within, echoing throughout the churchyard. All at once, the crowd turned, eyes widening in terror, their garbled shouts shrieking with the wind, fading into forward screams.

"Witch!" Widow Hale screeched, blood streaking her ears, her cry sharp as she pointed a bony finger at Cassandra's haggard form looming at the forest's edge. Torches flared, fists raised, mud sucked at tattered boots, the crowd's fear a blade plunging into her gut. She froze, drowned in confusion.

Why do they hate me? My voice...has it cursed them?

She returned to the circle, her body young again within its border, but her terror remained, the accusations a weight too heavy to carry. Her breath turned ragged as she sank to her knees, struggling to piece it all together — the reversed plea, the terrified gazes, the pointed fingers. *Blood takes her.* The words had stained her lips, a reversed chant she gave unwillingly, sparking the townsfolk's dread, naming her mother a witch. Realization seized her, freezing her in place until her marrow splintered like the cracked surface of an icy lake: She was the specter, her shadow the flame that lit the pyre. Guilt flooded her once more, heavier than the mud that sucked at her limbs, dragged her to the circle's center as her father had been wrangled before the Natives who cursed her to this place. And yet, hope lingered still, a resilient ember unwilling to die in the damp and rot that surrounded her. Images of her mother unburned, her eyes alive, her voice a soft song curling inside her ears plucked at her heartstrings. Perhaps she simply had not gone far enough back in time. If she reached further back, warned them before the accusations, could she save her mother then? She clung to the circle, its ash a lifeline, vowing to learn its rule, to save Iris before the fire took her.

Time snapped.

The village flickered, dusk bleeding into day, the rain lifting from the ground, absorbing back into the clouds from where they'd fallen. Widow Hale's reversed cry returned to her mouth, her accusing finger curling back to her palm, reaching away from Iris. Villagers ceased their fighting, fists unclenching, blood retreating from mud that smoothed back beneath their boots. Cassandra's mother rejoined the crowd, her slurred chant slipping back, unspoken, unnecessary.

"Kcab yats!"

A younger Cassandra removed herself from her mother, shawl untangling, her scream bending backward. "Reh s'ti!" She looked on helplessly from within the circle, the elder's chant pulsing in her veins. *Blood calls blood.* Outside, time unraveled, the world slipping backward as torches became unlit, shouts became unheard, accusations became unborn. She remained a specter in the shadows, glimpsed only at night, a shadow cast by the cursed ground. When she had stepped out at the pyre, she had aged herself, sown fear with her chant. She knew that she had caused the madness that followed, but still, hope burned, a stubborn light that refused to be snuffed out. If she had warned them earlier, before Hale's cry, could she have stopped it all?

Memories of her mother flooded once more, the warmth of her voice a needed respite from the dark, damp chill of the circle's grasp. They had run from Danvers, run from the whispers of an unseen witch. Cassandra stiffened, a tingle threading through her spine as the thought sprouted in her gut, a tangle of roots twisting into her intestines.

Had I brought those whispers here?

The circle's ash pulsed once more, pulling her back to the elder's hands smearing symbols across her face beneath a bitter moon, her eyes heavy with judgment. Cassandra had taken her father's place, bound to this backward hell. She clutched her shawl, the threads as frayed as her resolve, the vow to reach further back clawing to the surface of her mind. If she could find the moment before fear took root, could she save her mother before the village turned on her?

Time snapped.

The homestead loomed, the night's shroud lifting, mildew shrinking back into a reverse blossom from its sagging boards, the air freshening, no longer reeking of bitter rot. Cassandra remained within the circle, twigs rejoining beyond the rim as the earth thawed, no longer cracked by decay. She saw herself by the hearth, the scream stuffed back into her mouth, her face no longer warped by a frostbitten windowpane, the remnants of cold melting off its glassy surface. When she'd stepped out of the circle before, time had aged her, skin sagging, hair white, the very image of the hag that she'd seen by the river. She had scared her younger self, her cry fading into silence now the longer she remained in the circle. Her shadow had sown dread, a specter glimpsed by candlelight, but earlier, she could warn herself, remove the nightmares before whispers of witches crept in.

Guilt coiled tighter, a vice around her heart, yet that persistent hope burned brighter still. She sank to the circle's center, fingers tracing the ash where her father's knees had been planted, its warmth a faint echo of the ritual's fire. Iris's face flickered, her smile by the wagon, her voice steady.

"Cassie, you're my steel." Had she shattered that steel, led her to the stake?

The wilds outside pressed away, the pines no longer claws raking a violent sky, their shadows slipping away from the dusk. Cassandra watched them, studied them, the desperation mounting in her soul, holding her captive like the ancient stones that jailed her to the circle. She had seen her mother unburned, her eyes alive; there had to be a way to preserve her, return the life that had been stolen the same way the pines bloomed afresh beyond her prison.

"Blood calls blood." The elder's chant pulsed louder, a warning or a guide, and she clung to them, vowing to find the moment to save her mother before the world took her again.

Time snapped.

The church gleamed, its steeple unmarking the sky, moss stilling over its frame, the air no longer weighted with sermons. Cassandra stood rooted in the circle, watching her family step backwards from the Collins's homily, their boots retracting from the mud. The reverend's voice reversed with time.

"Eltbus skrul live." The twisted hymn snagged her skull, his words unspoken, unheard, yet still a scar worn raw upon her heart. She raised her hand, tears glinting, breath clouding in misty plumes through the circle. Outside, her specter haunted them, a shadow unseen but heavy, cast by the ritual's strange air. She'd aged at the pyre, scared them at the homestead, but here, before sermons of evil, could she warn her mother, remove the seeds of fear?

Memories surged, her mother's hand on her shoulder, guiding her through the church's dim light. "Stay close, Cassie," she had whispered, her voice a shield against the wilds' secrets. She'd felt safe then, had she not? Before the river, before the shadows. Had she brought those shadows here, her fear the spark that lit her mother's pyre?

The circle's ash pulsed, a heartbeat under her boots as she sank to her knees once more, clutching her bloodstained shawl, the scarlet splatters a map of her failures. She'd chanted at the fire, aged herself, and become the witch the crowd had feared. But earlier, before Collins's sermon, she could speak, undo the curse before it took hold. Hope flickered, a fragile flame against the guilt that wracked her as she vowed to find her mother again, save her before the world unmade her.

Time snapped.

The creek shimmered, its trickle unfading against the pines' rustle, humidity lifting from the air, herbs unwilted with the crisp breeze. Iris lifted from her knees, the sage and yarrow returned to the earth beneath, her skirt unstained by the damp soil. A younger Cassandra stood by, her gaze pulled away from the swaying moss, her frame unbent by the riverbank. Within the circle, she stood, cloak dragging, hands trembling, eyes burning with fresh tears. Outside, she heard her mother's voice calling.

"Esolc yats." The reversed command was a taunt unspoken. Cassandra's shadow stretched, the moment yet untainted by her presence, but Iris was alive, her hands unbloodied, her laughter untouched by flames. If she stepped outside the circle, endured the aging, she could warn her here before the whispers of witches reached her, before the fire's shadow fell. She scampered to the circle's edge, fingers digging into the ash as hope surged, the sight of her mother unburned, unbound igniting in her chest.

"You're my light, Cassie." Her mother's words tugged at her heart, burned in her skull, a vow she had betrayed. She'd run from shadows at the river, by the pines, her fear the seed of terror that fueled the flames that licked her mother's flesh. The world outside slipped further back as time unraveled once more. She'd chanted at the pyre, scared her younger self at the homestead, loomed too heavy at Collins's sermon, but here, surely here, by the creek's gentle flow, she could speak, unmake the fear before it took her.

Time snapped.

The river gleamed, its ragged voice clawing at her bones, the mist dissipating from the air. Cassandra saw herself once more by the riverbank, her limbs no longer flailing, eyes no longer widening with fear, the terror fading as she scrambled backward through time, her racing legs returning to a leisurely pace. She stood within the circle, heart pounding, cloak sodden with mud, the ash pulsing beneath her boots as the realization smacked her yet again. Here, too, she had reached for herself and failed, had she not? That last ember of hope fizzled away as the guilt drowned her yet again, but she needed to try. She stepped from the circle, time devouring her, skin sagging, hair graying, voice rasping raw.

"Break it!" she cried, hand raised through time, but the madness choked her, that same curse swallowing her words. "Rheh-seh-kat doolb." Her younger self belted in fear, the sound piercing her skull with the terror she'd sown. She chased herself, wild, unmoored, desperate to save herself, to save her mother, not trying to terrorize. Her steps thudded heavily, voice a ragged whisper unheard. Despair sank deep as she watched her younger self flee, the sight of it loosening a bitter laugh from her chest, the sound cracking around a frustrated sob, the tears and anguish blending in a howl that shook her frame. She'd tried to warn herself — at the pyre, the village, the creek — each time, her voice a twisted reversal, sowing dread where she'd meant to plant hope. The very specter she had feared had been within her all along, her shadow the spark that lit her mother's pyre. Only her death could stop the cycle.

Time snapped.

Danvers flickered, years forward, a cart's splintered belly piecing itself back together, the wood reconnecting under rain that fell upward toward a brightening sky. Her younger self cried out, the backwards slur burrowing itself back inside her chest.

"Rehtom!"

Blood retracted back into Iris's untorn nailbeds, the scarlet stains disappearing from her skirt, her belly swelling with a sister no longer stillborn from the crowd's chaos. The vow that Cassandra had carried spilled in a distorted scream from her mother's lips as she watched and listened from within the circle.

"Ssac, nur!"

She'd reached too far back, her shadow tainting the moment, unseen but heavy. With every undone cry, every unmade memory, the realization of her failure knotted itself tighter in her chest. The river, the pyre, the chaos in Danvers — it mattered not the moment in time. Her destiny had been written, and no warning she tried to give could erase it.

The truth clawed up, cruel and slow: every moment, every scream had been her fault. Not Jacob, not Margaret — Cassandra. Iris burned, villagers fought, Earnest broke, all because of her reach, her shadow. Every pyre, every accusation, she'd woven it, that terrible chant escaping from her throat, unbidden, unwilling.

"Rheh-seh-kat doolb." *Blood takes her.*

Tears dripped in crimson streaks down her face, warm and thick, pooling on her lips, bitter as the iron she'd tasted in the clearing. She laughed, quiet at first, then loud, a cracked rasp splitting the silence, a howl born of madness, her hands clawing her face, nails tearing skin until scarlet swelled, warm and fading.

"Me, always me!" she croaked, voice wild, breaking under the weight of the truth. Madness bloomed, a hunger gnawing her bones, the Wendigo's curse hers alone, its claws sharper than the guilt that tore her heart to shreds. The laugh grew, a requiem breaking the dark, her head tilting back, neck popping as she staggered, the circle's ash pulsing as though the soot at her feet were alive.

She crawled into a nearby cave, its jagged walls a mural of moss and decay, a tomb vibrating with her past, the air thick with damp and rot. Her cloak shredded, mud dragging at her hem, threads unraveling like the hope that had been extinguished, the final ember guttering out to blackness.

"End it, end me," she begged, that stubborn chant spilling forth instead. "Rheh-seh-kat doolb." The rhythm of her words echoed the river's snarl, a curse she'd cast unto herself. Iris's pyre blazed in her skull, her unburned form a hope she'd betrayed, her laughter by the creek, her hands braiding Cassandra's hair, all of it ash, all of it a cruel dream flickering to darkness.

She grasped at the vines that surrounded her, hands trembling, lifting her frail frame as the circle's soot blossomed at her feet. The memories flooded once more, this time she listened carefully, her mother's guidance at the wagon's wheel a lesson woven through nimble fingers.

"Steady, Cassie." The vow twisted in her gut as she tied the noose, the vines coarse, their fibers biting her palms, a mirror to the guilt devouring her soul. She'd seen her younger self fleeing by the river, her eyes wide with fear she'd sown, her scream a blade in her skull. Her shadow had lit the pyre, each attempt — the pyre, the village, the river — another iteration of that cursed chant, that horrid hex that had named her mother a witch. She'd scared her, driven the mob's fire, woven their fear with her voice, her reach, her blood.

"It's the only way to stop me," she whispered, eyes steadfast on the river's gleam, the fleeting sparkle across its surface a mirror to the hope she'd lost. The noose tightened, a void clawing at her soul, damnation waiting, a limbo unseen but heavy as the air that bound her to this hell. Her neck snapped, breath faded, laughter a mournful whisper in the cave's damp, unanswered by the wilds beyond. Darkness rushed, her eyes glazed, the witch born, hanging eternal, her soul sinking to a nothingness she'd earned, her mother's face the final image, unburned, untaken — a light she clung to as the world faded to black.

Chapter 17

Boots squelched along mud-soaked earth as Collins stepped past the square, past the churchyard, eyes fixed on the forest's edge, gaze stubbornly rooted to the skeletal pines that stretched their jagged fingers upward to a smoke-colored haze. Though the stake had long since been dismantled, Iris's blackened remains shoveled away beneath the muck and mire that tugged at the soles of his feet, he made a point not to linger where her body had been burned — not since that night in the circle.

Light flashed in his mind, that guttural howl grating his nerves as piercing now as it had been beneath the silver moon, Cassandra's fragile frame there one moment, gone the next, a specter folded into the wind that carried her cries. The reverend had seen it all, had listened to Earnest's broken pleas as he clawed the ash and blood, filth burrowing beneath his fingernails as though he could unearth his daughter from the circle that had claimed her.

"Cass!" he had screamed, over and over, his sea-weathered voice as frayed as the ropes that dangled in loose knots from his wrists, the twine tattered and tangled at his knees that crushed the earth with the weight of his loss. Collins had stood by him, a shadow looming heavy at his side, not a sermon to spare nor comfort to offer that could quell the sailor's grief. Even if he had the words to stem the tide of despair, the priest knew they'd mean nothing, a hollow sentiment stained in untold guilt, Margaret's flush gnawing at his soul, Jacob's laughter rustling through the Spanish moss that swayed with the song of his escape.

Earnest had left Charleston not long after that night, his pain and guilt a fire burning bright in his soul, a reflection of the pyre that had claimed his wife, the light that had stolen his daughter in the circle. There were no goodbyes to be had, no tear-streaked faces mourning his absence when dawn came and shone its dull, gray light upon the empty homestead. The town carried the knowledge of his departure the same way they carried the shame of their role in what had driven him away — not a stain to cloak from prying eyes, but a badge of honor to be displayed, a promise to do the same to any evil that dared to lurk where their children wandered in the trees. Talk of the Yorks' eradication traveled in hushed whispers, a quiet chant that echoed through the square like an incantation.

"Witch's kin no more."

"Drove them away for good."

"Evil's been cast out."

But while the townsfolk rejoiced at the fate of the Yorks, guilt weighed heavy around the reverend's neck, a slipknot tightening around his throat, constricting his breath with each passing day since the night of the circle's curse. His mind snagged on the words from his sermon weeks past, the message more a prophecy than a homily, coiling in his eardrum with the same incessant pull of the river.

"Evil lurks subtle."

He thought of Margaret, the scrape of her wheezing grating on his ears in the stillness of the night, her eyes glassy and cold, devoid of the unnatural vigor that had bled from her irises and transformed her complexion. Ever since Jacob had slipped into the trees, she had become a ghost of herself, her rosy glow extinguished with the embers that had sent smoke curling up to the sky on the day Iris was burned. Collins could not ignore the connection, nor the way his wife gazed longingly out the window of their cottage, eyes trained on the forest, as if searching for that crooked grin through the trees. She did not speak his name, but the priest could see it written in the way her skin faded to gray in Jacob's absence, could hear it whispered in the ragged breaths that chafed her lungs with each day that passed without another child's disappearance. He hated the desperation in her eyes, how it seeped from her pores and snaked through the house, planting its seeds inside him until he, too, found his mind wandering to the trees, hope and fear dueling in his chest each time he saw a shadow dart between the branches, heard a rustling breeze that sounded too much like laughter.

"Lord, forgive me," he muttered as he pressed onward through the forest, coat pulled tight around his shaking frame to fend off the chill that fell beneath the canopy of bent pines. Penance had become a ritual in the days that followed Jacob's retreat, Earnest's departure, Cassandra's curse. And so it was that he'd trek into the woods to that circle of ancient stones, head bowed with the branches that swallowed the sky overhead, prayers stained on wrinkled lips as he sought forgiveness from a god that granted nothing more than silence in return.

It had been weeks of this routine, the dead leaves and twigs now a well-worn path from the pastor's cabin to the circle of stones in the heart of the forest. Though he'd traveled the road through the wood each day, his boot prints in the mud a map more recognizable to him now than the veins that sprawled like blue spiderwebs on the back of his hand, it wasn't until this particular venture through the pines that he saw the mouth of the cave, its toothless maw beckoning to him from the circle's edge. Something raw and ancient tugged at his marrow, pulled him closer to the ebony opening despite the reek of decay that spilled from the craggy entrance like a warning. Dread curdled in his abdomen as his toes breached the threshold, the stench of rot clinging to the stone walls in a blanket of damp that chilled his bones more than the bite of the wind that whistled in mournful groans through the cracks in the cavern.

Death clawed at his nostrils, the sickly sweet must choking his throat as he stepped deeper into the tunnel, his need to find the source of the smell bewitching his mind, erasing all reason, all desire to turn and run back to the safety of his cottage. Slowly, the cave devoured him, his eyes straining against the dim, gray light that grew meeker with every step. A scream died in his lungs, the breath stolen from his chest as he stumbled into a black mass, its pendulous rhythm rocking back to graze his body once more, the weight of it sending him backward to seek purchase on the rocky walls that surrounded him. His eyes strained through the frail light, vision sharpening with his realization as he blinked through the darkness and saw the horror staring back at him.

"What hell is this?" His hoarse whisper echoed off the stone, the chorus of his fear swaying with the dangling limbs of the hanging corpse suspended before him. Mud-caked cloaks fell like spectral shadows around wrinkled skin, a crown of white hair flowing down a crooked neck snapped and mangled by the vines that choked the life from the old woman that floated like a forgotten ghost ravaged by time. His heart sank, the ache of a shepherd who'd lost another of his flock to darkness untold, a priest whose sermons had fallen on ears already charmed by the devil's forked tongue.

"My child." His breath hitched around a broken sob as he stepped closer to the hanging woman, his fingers searching through the shadows to untangle the vines that kept her suspended. "There is no rest to be had here. I will lay you down, give you to the earth, so you may have your slumber in the loving arms of our Lord."

He looked around the cave floor until he came upon a rock, the jagged edge reminding him of that whalebone hilt that had ended Tala's life in the shack beside the river. The reverend cast the images from his mind, focusing on the serrated teeth of stone chewing through vine as he loosened the corpse from its noose. He coughed around the cloud of decay that plumed up his nostrils as he cradled the body in his arms and carried her into the clearing, tears streaking through the grime on his wrinkled cheeks, spilling down onto the threadbare shawl wrapped around the lifeless limbs. In the center of the circle, he set the body down, kneeling beside it to claw at the earth — the same way that Earnest had in the aftermath of his daughter's disappearance.

Echoes of the sailor's despair filled his ears as he worked the soil, nails cracking in the dirt, blood mixing with the mud and ash as he dug deeper until he sat crouched in the center of a shallow grave. He raised himself on creaking knees, boots slipping in the damp as he scurried up the side of the hole to join the corpse on solid ground. Gently, he rolled the body into its final resting place before standing up, head bowed in reverent lament as he whispered the words to a quiet eulogy, a somber service that only the pines would witness.

"Grant, O Lord, that we who yet remain may so number our days that we apply our hearts unto wisdom, living soberly, righteously, and godly in this present world, that, when our own hour shall come, we may be found in faith and peace, ready to enter into Thy heavenly rest."

As he knelt once more to the earth, sinking his hands into the soil to blanket the body in dirt, the branches swayed overhead. Had it not been for the grunts of his labor as he buried yet another of God's lost children, he would have heard the distinct sound of that vile laughter singing through the wind, telling of secrets still hidden, of curses still kept dormant somewhere in the cover of darkness.

Epilogue

The rope's coarse bite dissolved into a tide of ecstasy, vast and unmoored, flooding Cassandra's veins with a pulse she had not felt since girlhood, when the world was still soft, unscarred, its edges yet to sharpen into blades. Her vision swam, bright and fractured, light seared through the dark, a blinding slash that clawed her eyes 'til they watered, tears streaking warm and thick down her cheeks, tasting of salt and something older, something iron-sharp that lingered on her tongue. She'd stepped into death beneath a shroud of night, the grove's damp rot had consumed her last breath, yet now a day blazed before her. More radiant and pure than anything she had ever witnessed.

Its glare a mockery of the Hell she'd braced for. No flames licked her skin, no sulfur choked her lungs. The air hung crisp, crystalline, alive, carrying a breeze that rustled like whispers through a valley unfurling vast and wild: mountains stabbed the sky, their peaks glinting jagged as broken teeth; trees swayed, their leaves shimmering like glass kissed by frost.

A river snaked below, its surface molten, flashing with a light that burned her hollowed gaze. What was this place? It is sublime. The ground beneath her boots crunched, dry grass snapping faint, not the mud she'd clawed through, its scent sharp with pine and a sweetness that was so pure that it felt as if she was consuming honey with every breath she took.

"Cassandra?" a voice sliced the stillness, clear, trembling, jarring her spine like a bell that had been struck too hard. She turned, slow, her cloak dragging heavy, its tattered hem snagging on the earth, mud flaking dry in clots that crumbled under her weight. There, Iris, running toward her, not the weary woman of Charleston's pyre. Her skirt charred and eyes steel-sharp, but young, radiant, her dark hair spilling loose, unmarred by soot, her face unlined, glowing with a vigor the stake had burned away. Her skirt flared as she moved, clean, untorn, her bare feet silent on the grass, her breath fogging faint in the chill that should not have been there. It was in that moment Cassandra asked herself if this was this Heaven?

"Oh, Cassandra! What are you doing here?" Iris's voice quavered, joy clashing with fear, her hands reaching out, trembling as they hovered near Cassandra's face, as if afraid she'd shatter at the touch.

"Mother?" Cassandra's throat tightened, her voice rasped, a cracked shard scraping her lungs, the words spilling like blood from a wound too deep. "I...I hanged myself. To end

it." Her hands shook, gnarled now, nails split and crusted with blood, the noose's memory a phantom weight around her neck, its fibers still prickling her skin as if it was still hanging around her neck. She swayed, breath hitching, her cloak sagging, heavy with the grove's damp, its rot clinging faint beneath the valley's purity, a stain she could not shed.

Iris's face crumpled, her eyes widened, wet with a grief that cut sharper than a blade. "I was just burned at the stake, moments ago, the smoke still in my lungs. You should not be here." She seized Cassandra's hands, warm against her cold, her grip iron-tight, fingers digging into flesh as if to anchor her daughter to this impossible place. Her breath hitched, her gaze darted over Cassandra, tracing the gray strands snarled in her hair, the sagging skin beneath her eyes, the blood streaking faint from their corners. "What happened to you?"

"It was me," Cassandra blurted, her voice broke, raw and wild, the confession clawing free like a beast from its cage. "I caused it. All of it! Some how..... I went back, through time, I do not quite know how. There was a ritual to kill father. I tried to save him... I tried to save you.... I tried to warn you..." Cassandra could feel the lump coming up her throat. Eyes watering. "I tried to save you! I am so sorry! I tried."

Cassandra was now sobbing as she tried to explain this queer story to her mother. "The specter! The one chasing us. The townsfolk thought it was you, but it was me. It was not chasing us. I was trying to warn us. I damned you instead. I damned myself... I damned us all." Her chest heaved, tears falling down her cheeks and onto the dry grass below.

Cassandra was standing just feet away from Iris, but throwing her hands around and moving her body trying to explain everything she had been through. She stepped closer and grabbed her mother with a desperation she could not name. "Every scream, every pyre, I wove it you see. I reached through the dark, and they burned you for it. I was trying to help you. I was trying to save you. But they thought I was you."

Iris stared, her breath caught, uncomprehending, her hands tightened, bruising now, her voice fraying as she shook her head. "What specter? Cassandra, what do you mean?" Her eyes searched hers, steel flickering beneath confusion. Iris had just arrived from being burned alive, but yet felt like she had been here for centuries. What specter was Cassandra talking about? This story felt both familiar and foreign to Iris.

The valley's light shimmer began to quiver and quake as the soft beauty slowly rose into a tremulous ether. The river's hum slowly rose into a roar. A low snarl threading through the air. Something was tugging at Cassandra's bones with a hunger that gnawed deeper, a call she'd felt by the grove, by the river, in every shadow she'd cast. Something was not right.

The ground shuddered, sharp, visceral, earth cracking faint beneath her boots, a jolt that buckled her knees. She sank, mud surging through the dry grass. While the air was warm, the mud was cold around her calves, sucking wet and greedy, drowning the valley's sweetness. She no longer tasted honey but sulfur.

"Mother! Help me! What's happening?" Her voice tore, panic clawing her throat, her hands flailed, clawing at the soil, nails snapping off in jagged shards, blood streaking her fingers as the ground swallowed her shins, its grip tightening like a someone's hands wrapped around her legs. Slowly pulling her further and further down, hoping the mud would drown her. Consume her. Body and soul.

Iris lunged, her hands seizing Cassandra's arms, pulling with a strength she was confident she never had before. Iris', grunting and breathing heavy, "I know not! Hold fast!"

Cassandra's eyes darted up from her mother to the sky, then froze; widening with a dread that drained her face pale. A crowd had materialized out of seemingly nowhere. No sound or rustle, besides the roar of the entire valley. Just there. Thousands upon thousands of floating spirits, their forms hazy, drifting closer yet impossibly distant, a sea of silhouettes stretching to the horizon. They reminded her of her mother but more... pure. Millions now, faces blurred, eyes hollow, gazing skyward, locked in a rapture that chilled the air, their stillness a weight pressing Cassandra's chest 'til her ribs ached. The light and sound of the valley sounded like a holy battle cry that was majestic and terrifying.

"Help me!" Iris screamed, her voice cracked, a whip slashing the humming roar, her hands slipped, slick with Cassandra's blood as she pulled harder, boots digging ruts in the grass. "She's sinking!". Iris was too occupied attempting to save her daughter that she had not looked up but called out for help to both Cassandra and anyone that may be in earshot. Unknowingly to her, there seemed to be millions within earshot witnessing the events. No one stirred, the crowd's gaze held, unblinking, their silence a shroud thicker than the smoke of that Charleston's pyre that seems to have been a lifetime ago.

Cassandra clawed the earth, her waist engulfed now, mud seeping cold through her cloak, its weight dragging her deeper, her breath rasped, terror clawing her voice, "Mother, please!" Her arm stretched, trembling violent, fingers curling slow toward Iris, nails jagged and split, blood dripping to mingle with the mire.

"I'll be back," Iris vowed, her voice broke, a sob swallowed fast. She could feel a presence and was desperate to get help. Perhaps she could force someone to help. Perhaps she'd beg. Anything! It does not make sense why no one would help. She knew someone was close.

She released Cassandra, stumbling toward the nearest figure, a man, tall and gaunt, his face locked in rapt wonder, his cloak swaying faint as if caught in a wind she could not feel. She grabbed his arm, shaking him hard, her nails digging through fabric. "Help me! What's happening?" Her tone thundered, desperation cracking her steel, her hair whipped wild, streaked with sweat now, her breath quickening in the chill.

He turned, slow, deliberate, his eyes met hers, awe flattening to a hollow calm, his voice a monotone slicing the air like a blade through flesh. "Her soul is damned; she chose her fate. No one who murder's the Father's creation is welcome here." His words fell flat, cold, final, as if stating the hour, his gaze drifting back skyward, untroubled by the mud claiming her daughter, his hands limp at his sides, stained faint with blood that did not move him.

Iris staggered, breath seizing, her hands flew to her mouth, muffling a cry as she spun back. "No, Cassandra!" She lunged, too late, only Cassandra's head and one trembling arm jutted from the earth now, her fingers clawing air, reaching for her mother with a desperation that broke the valley's light. Mud kissed her chin, cold, wet, her eyes widened, blood streaking faint from their corners, tears mingling with the mire as she gasped, "Mother, do not leave," Her voice frayed, a shard swallowed by the ground's growl, the river's hum rising louder, a snarl weaving through her skull.

Iris dropped, knees slamming the grass, her hands clawed the mud, pulling frantic. "I wo not, I wo not!" she rasped, raw with a fury that defied the crowd's calm, her fingers sinking deep, slick with blood and earth as she fought the pull. She glanced up, up at whatever held the throng in thrall. She wondered what the man had stopped talking to her to look at but was too concerned with saving her daughter to look. But this time it fixed her eye. Her breath caught, eyes widening as a faint, euphoric hum rippled through the air, threading from the crowd like a soft chant. Her grip slackened, her body went limp, her face softened, iron melting to a vacant awe, her hands slipping free as she began to rise, drifting upward with the others, her cloak swaying faint, embers of her fire snuffed by a light she could not resist.

"No!" Cassandra's scream tore silent, trapped in her throat, mud surged over her mouth, choking her cry as her eyes burned, hollow and wild, glinting with a terror too deep. She understood, with a sharp cruelty, in that final, suffocating breath: It was not the curse that brought her here. The curse pushed her back through time, but she chose this fate. She not only was cursed to save her father, but she cursed herself to save everyone. Her guilt, her suicide a thread snapping her from grace, her soul a weight the valley could not hold.

The crowd's hum swelled, a dirge sealing her fate. Iris floated higher, her face serene, lost to a peace Cassandra could not touch. The light dimmed, the valley blurred, mud swallowed her eyes, her hand sinking last, fingers curling slow into the dark. She had been a specter damned by her own hand. She had now damned herself again, sinking alone into a void thick with the river's snarl and the echo of her mother's vow. Heaven was a hollow light she'd never reach.

She wondered why her. She was not of ill intent. Jacob, Margaret, the townsfolk, countless others were evil. She had tried to save those she loved. She even took her own life to make sure no one else died. Was this wrong? Had she misunderstood the rules of life? She may have taken the role of the classic witch but not for any personal gain. She knew she was good. And it appears the good are not rewarded. The good are damned. As everything slowly faded to black, she realized that she only belonged in hell. To be tortured with those other damned souls. As the cool black encompassed her body and soul she knew that she did not belong to our world nor the one beyond.

www.ingramcontent.com/pod-product-compliance
Lightning Source LLC
LaVergne TN
LVHW090522110826
845146LV00003B/953

* 9 7 9 8 9 9 4 6 5 6 4 1 9 *